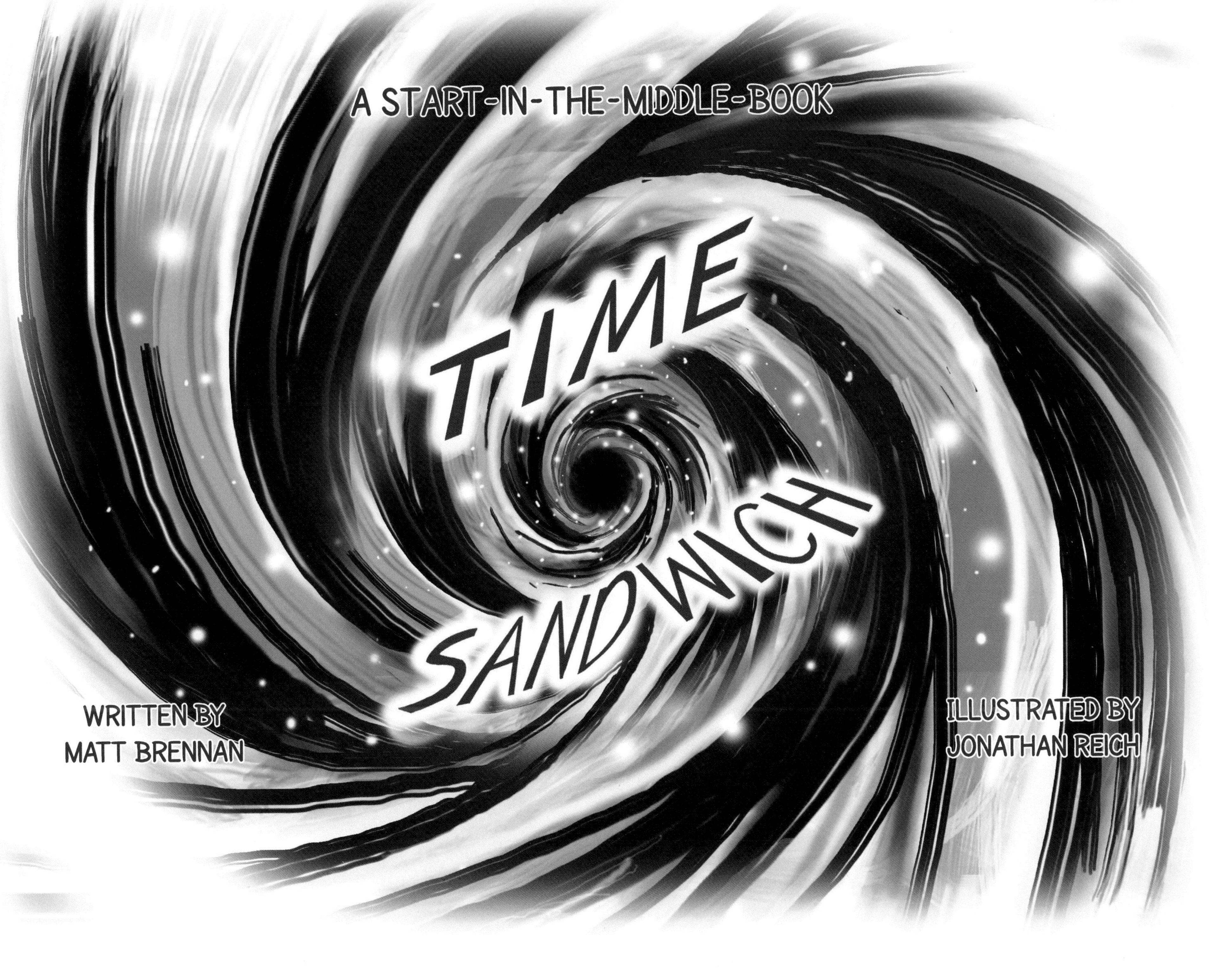

A START-IN-THE-MIDDLE-BOOK

TIME SANDWICH

WRITTEN BY
MATT BRENNAN

ILLUSTRATED BY
JONATHAN REICH

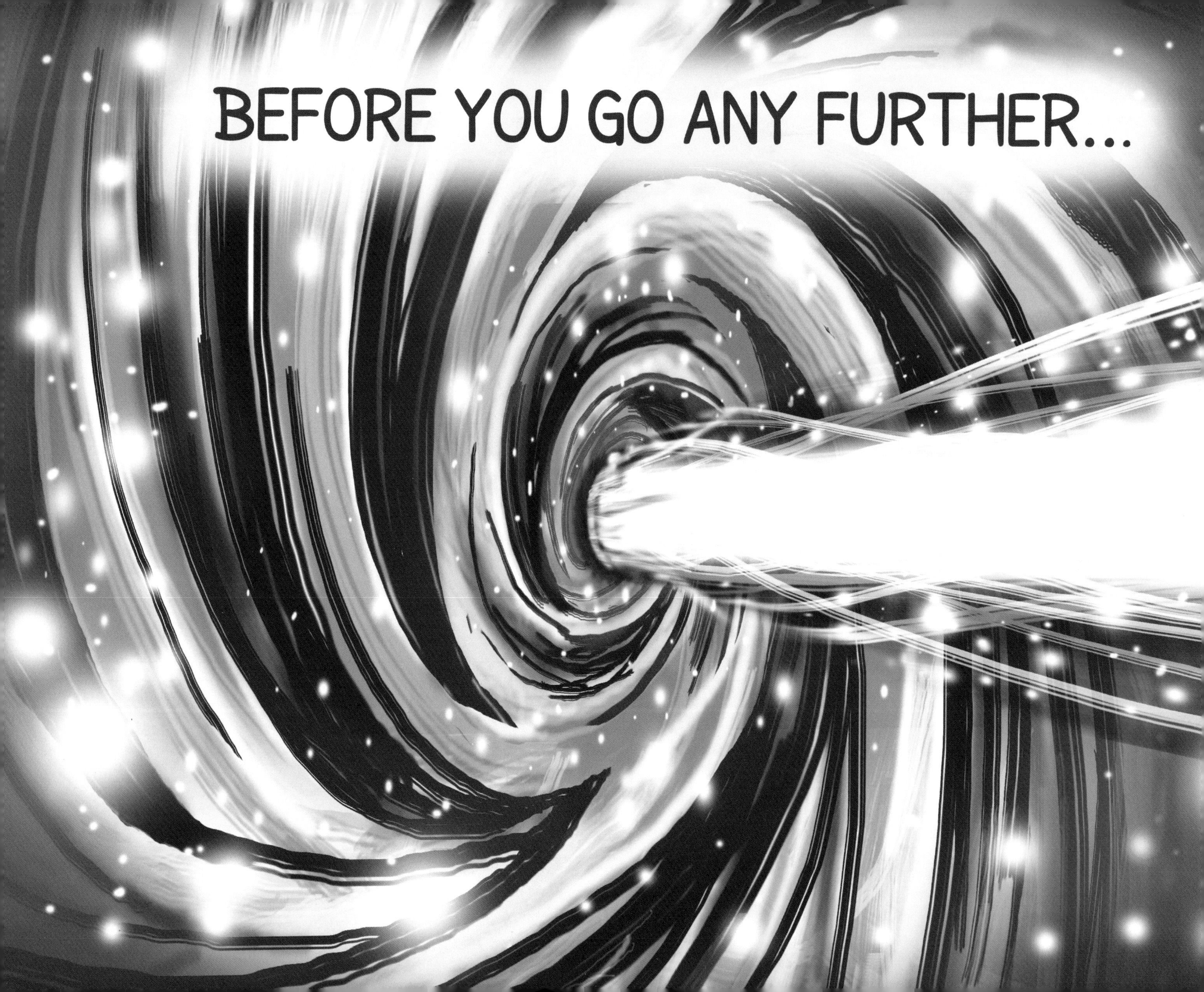
BEFORE YOU GO ANY FURTHER...

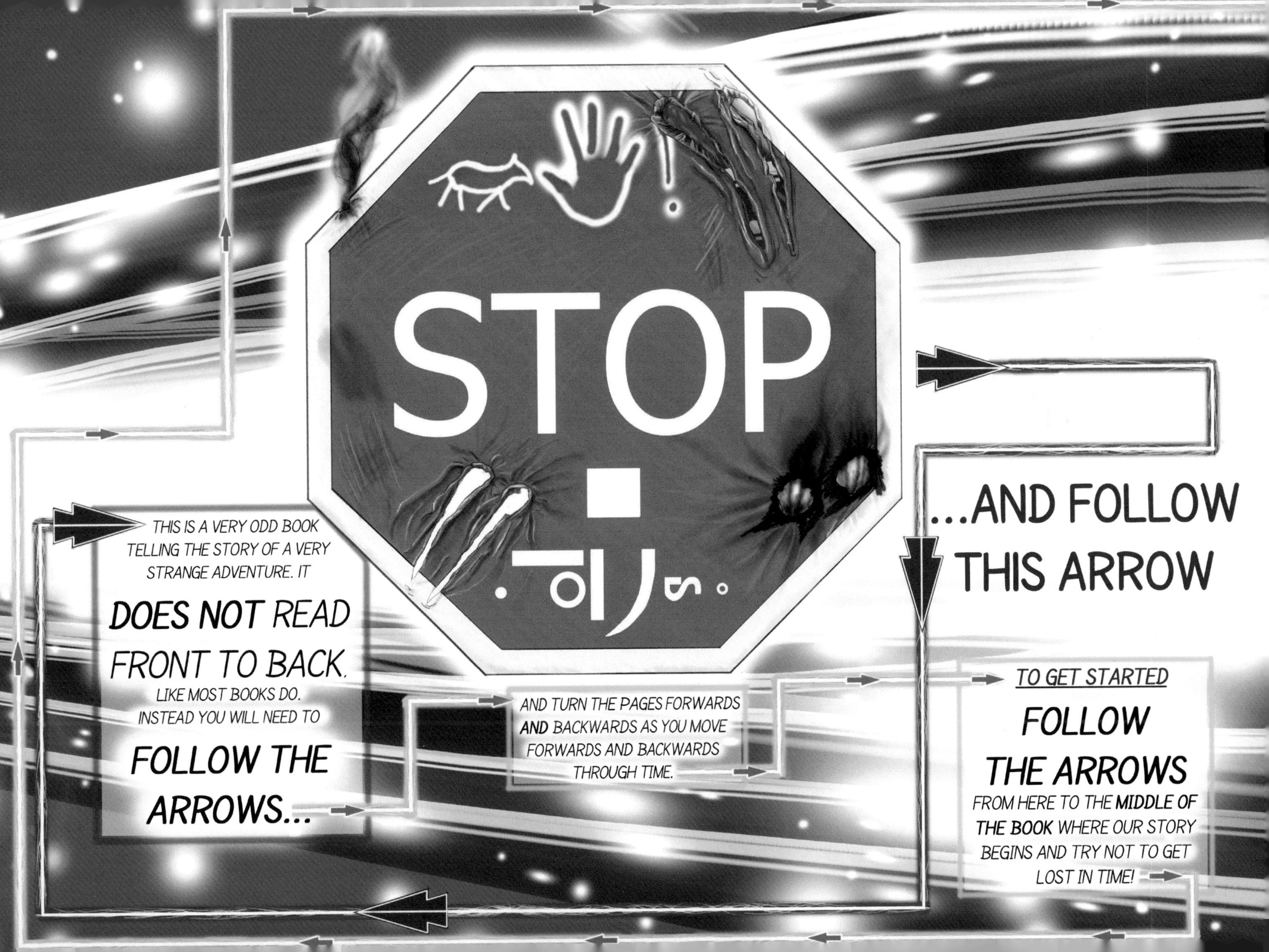
STOP
...AND FOLLOW THIS ARROW
THIS IS A VERY ODD BOOK TELLING THE STORY OF A VERY STRANGE ADVENTURE. IT
DOES NOT READ FRONT TO BACK,
LIKE MOST BOOKS DO. INSTEAD YOU WILL NEED TO
FOLLOW THE ARROWS...
AND TURN THE PAGES FORWARDS AND BACKWARDS AS YOU MOVE FORWARDS AND BACKWARDS THROUGH TIME.
TO GET STARTED
FOLLOW THE ARROWS
FROM HERE TO THE MIDDLE OF THE BOOK WHERE OUR STORY BEGINS AND TRY NOT TO GET LOST IN TIME!

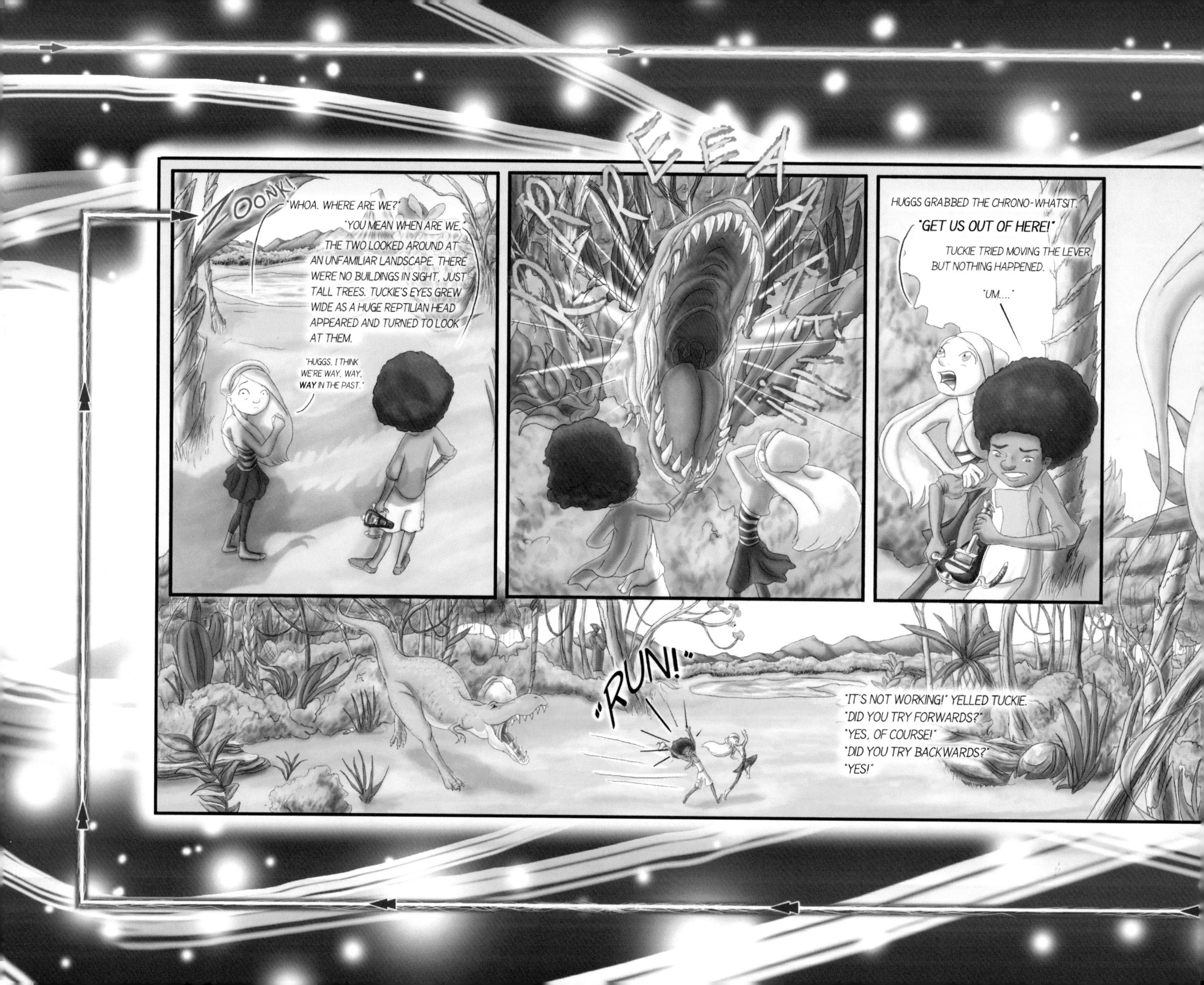
ZOONK!
"WHOA. WHERE ARE WE?"
"YOU MEAN WHEN ARE WE."
THE TWO LOOKED AROUND AT AN UNFAMILIAR LANDSCAPE. THERE WERE NO BUILDINGS IN SIGHT, JUST TALL TREES. TUCKIE'S EYES GREW WIDE AS A HUGE REPTILIAN HEAD APPEARED AND TURNED TO LOOK AT THEM.
"HUGGS, I THINK WE'RE WAY, WAY, **WAY** IN THE PAST."
HUGGS GRABBED THE CHRONO-WHATSIT.
"GET US OUT OF HERE!"
TUCKIE TRIED MOVING THE LEVER, BUT NOTHING HAPPENED.
"UM...."
"RUN!"
"IT'S NOT WORKING!" YELLED TUCKIE.
"DID YOU TRY FORWARDS?"
"YES, OF COURSE!"
"DID YOU TRY BACKWARDS?"
"YES!"

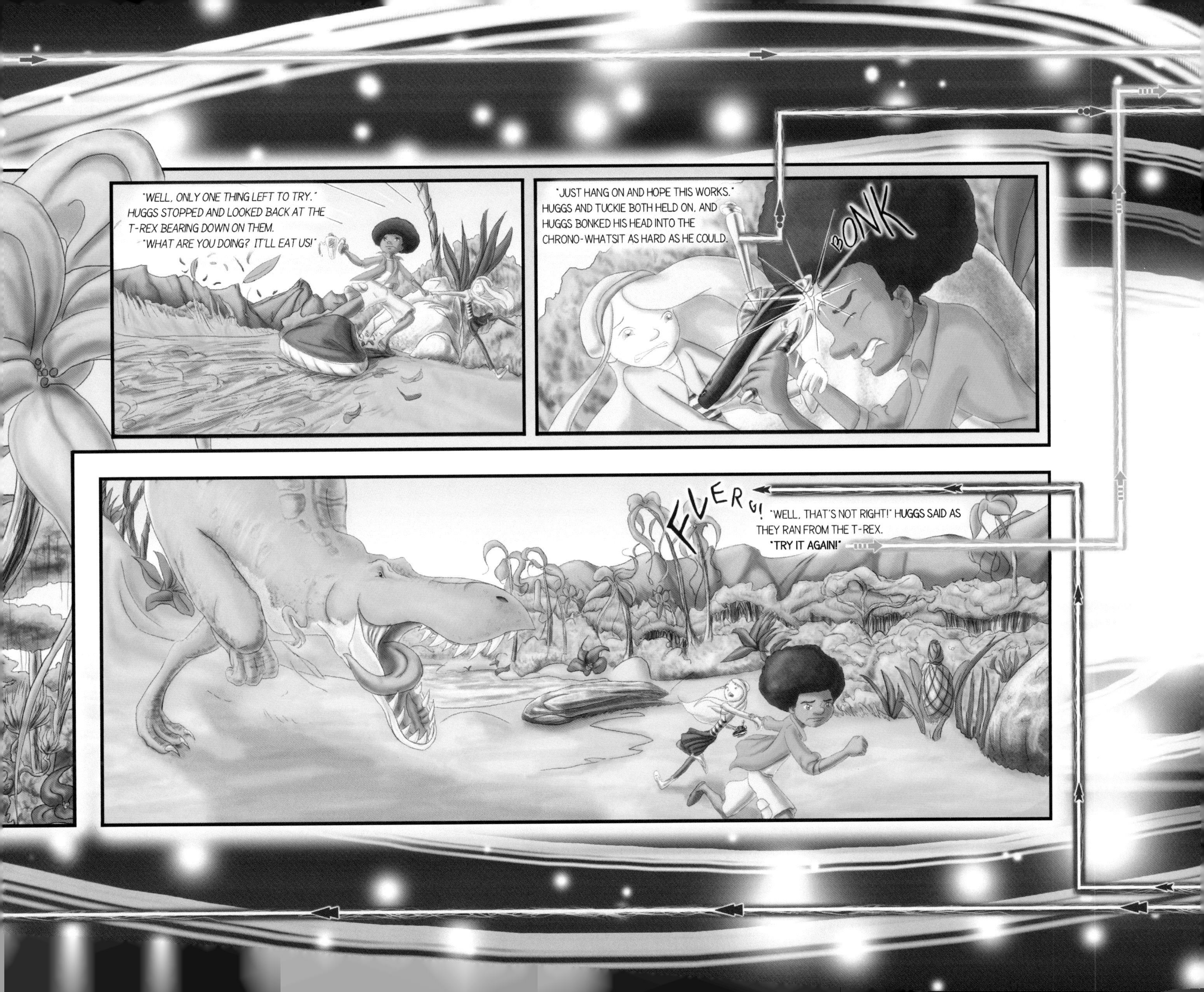
"WELL, ONLY ONE THING LEFT TO TRY." HUGGS STOPPED AND LOOKED BACK AT THE T-REX BEARING DOWN ON THEM.
"WHAT ARE YOU DOING? IT'LL EAT US!"
"JUST HANG ON AND HOPE THIS WORKS." HUGGS AND TUCKIE BOTH HELD ON, AND HUGGS BONKED HIS HEAD INTO THE CHRONO-WHATSIT AS HARD AS HE COULD.
BONK
FLERG!
"WELL, THAT'S NOT RIGHT!" HUGGS SAID AS THEY RAN FROM THE T-REX.
"TRY IT AGAIN!"

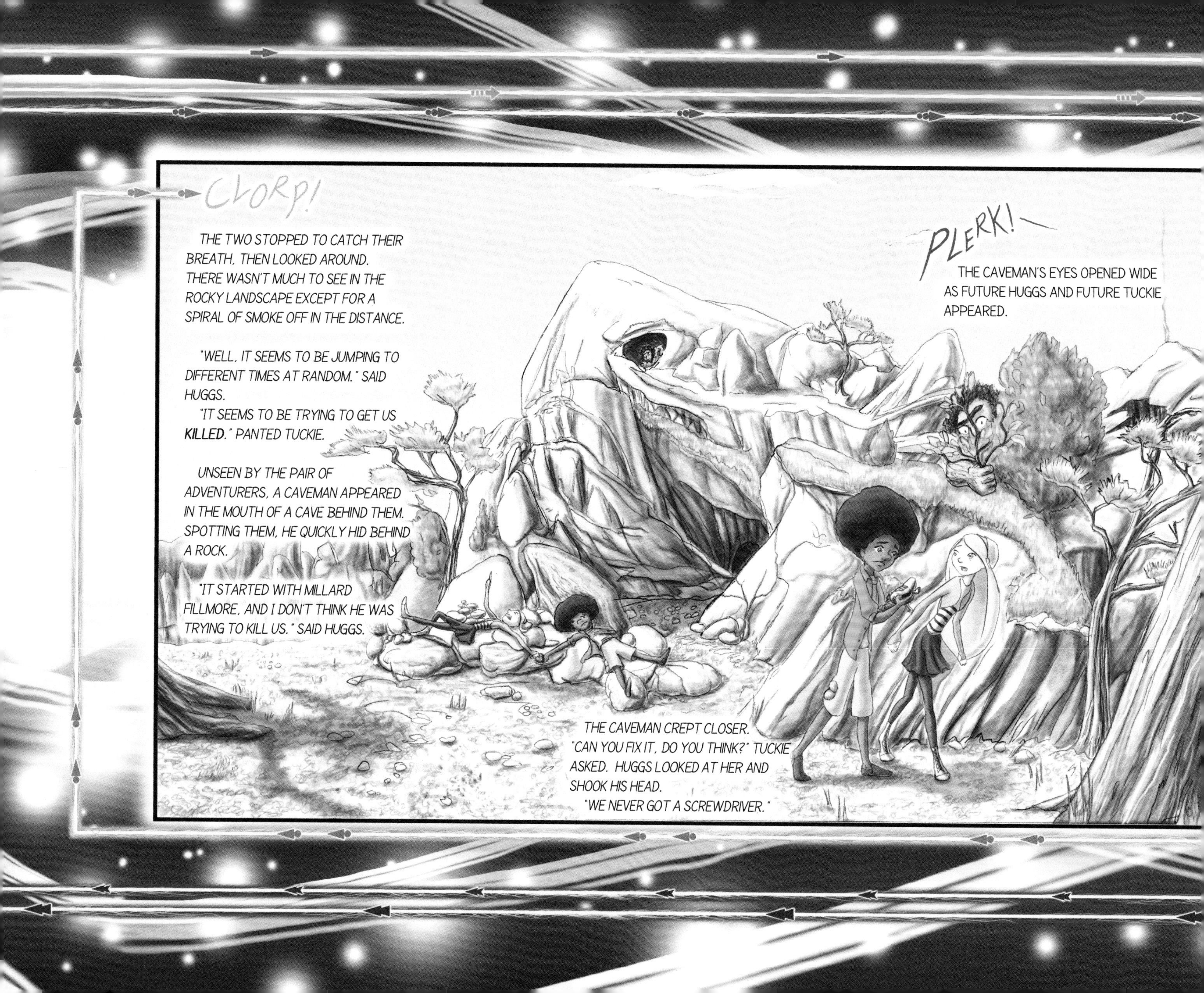

CLORP!
THE TWO STOPPED TO CATCH THEIR BREATH, THEN LOOKED AROUND. THERE WASN'T MUCH TO SEE IN THE ROCKY LANDSCAPE EXCEPT FOR A SPIRAL OF SMOKE OFF IN THE DISTANCE.
"WELL, IT SEEMS TO BE JUMPING TO DIFFERENT TIMES AT RANDOM." SAID HUGGS.
"IT SEEMS TO BE TRYING TO GET US **KILLED.**" PANTED TUCKIE.
UNSEEN BY THE PAIR OF ADVENTURERS, A CAVEMAN APPEARED IN THE MOUTH OF A CAVE BEHIND THEM. SPOTTING THEM, HE QUICKLY HID BEHIND A ROCK.
"IT STARTED WITH MILLARD FILLMORE, AND I DON'T THINK HE WAS TRYING TO KILL US." SAID HUGGS.
PLERK!
THE CAVEMAN'S EYES OPENED WIDE AS FUTURE HUGGS AND FUTURE TUCKIE APPEARED.
THE CAVEMAN CREPT CLOSER.
"CAN YOU FIX IT, DO YOU THINK?" TUCKIE ASKED. HUGGS LOOKED AT HER AND SHOOK HIS HEAD.
"WE NEVER GOT A SCREWDRIVER."

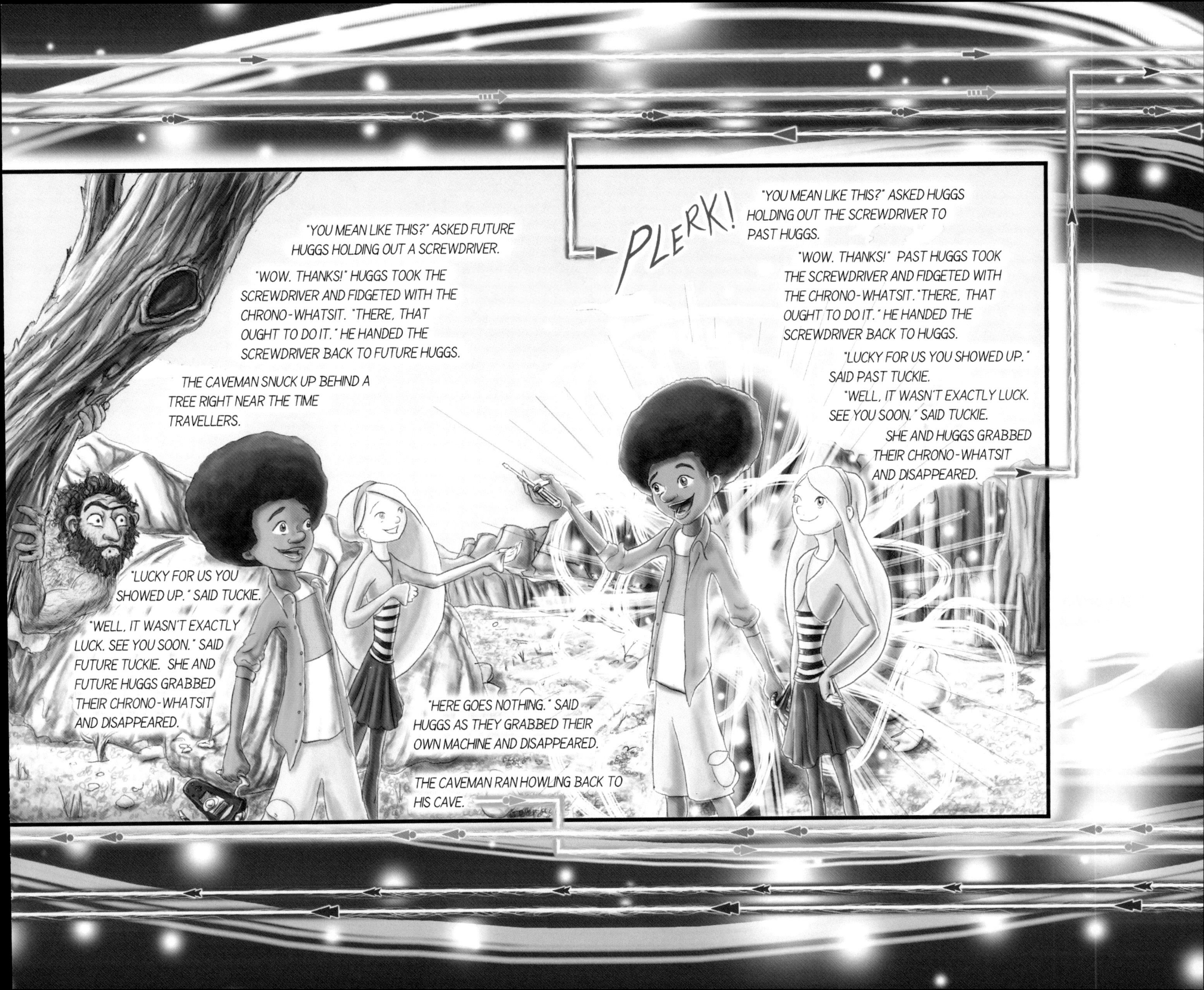
"YOU MEAN LIKE THIS?" ASKED FUTURE HUGGS HOLDING OUT A SCREWDRIVER.
"WOW. THANKS!" HUGGS TOOK THE SCREWDRIVER AND FIDGETED WITH THE CHRONO-WHATSIT. "THERE, THAT OUGHT TO DO IT." HE HANDED THE SCREWDRIVER BACK TO FUTURE HUGGS.
THE CAVEMAN SNUCK UP BEHIND A TREE RIGHT NEAR THE TIME TRAVELLERS.
"LUCKY FOR US YOU SHOWED UP." SAID TUCKIE.
"WELL, IT WASN'T EXACTLY LUCK. SEE YOU SOON." SAID FUTURE TUCKIE. SHE AND FUTURE HUGGS GRABBED THEIR CHRONO-WHATSIT AND DISAPPEARED.
"HERE GOES NOTHING." SAID HUGGS AS THEY GRABBED THEIR OWN MACHINE AND DISAPPEARED.
THE CAVEMAN RAN HOWLING BACK TO HIS CAVE.
PLERK!
"YOU MEAN LIKE THIS?" ASKED HUGGS HOLDING OUT THE SCREWDRIVER TO PAST HUGGS.
"WOW. THANKS!" PAST HUGGS TOOK THE SCREWDRIVER AND FIDGETED WITH THE CHRONO-WHATSIT. "THERE, THAT OUGHT TO DO IT." HE HANDED THE SCREWDRIVER BACK TO HUGGS.
"LUCKY FOR US YOU SHOWED UP." SAID PAST TUCKIE.
"WELL, IT WASN'T EXACTLY LUCK. SEE YOU SOON." SAID TUCKIE.
SHE AND HUGGS GRABBED THEIR CHRONO-WHATSIT AND DISAPPEARED.

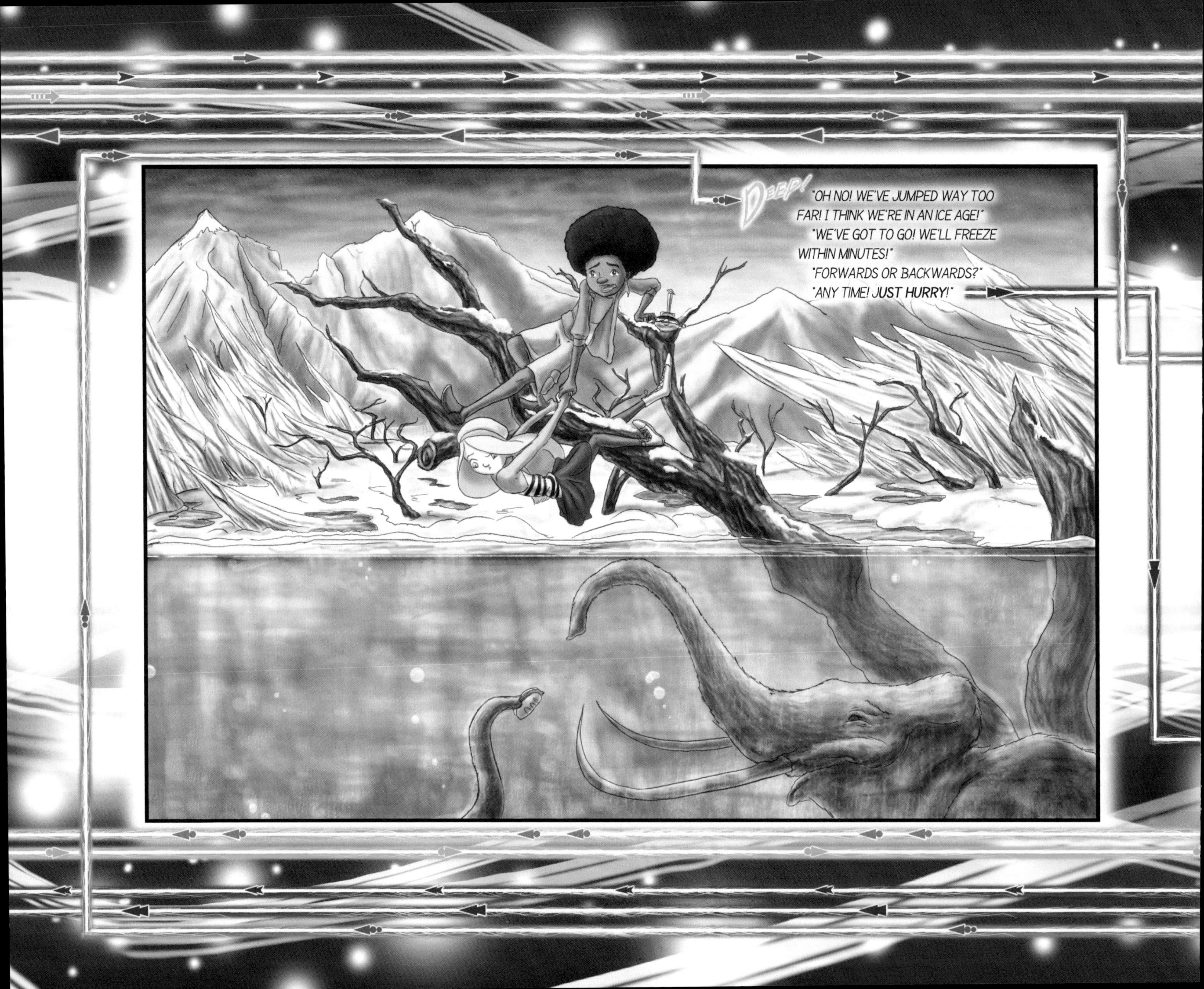
DEEP!
"OH NO! WE'VE JUMPED WAY TOO FAR! I THINK WE'RE IN AN ICE AGE!"
"WE'VE GOT TO GO! WE'LL FREEZE WITHIN MINUTES!"
"FORWARDS OR BACKWARDS?"
"ANY TIME! JUST HURRY!"

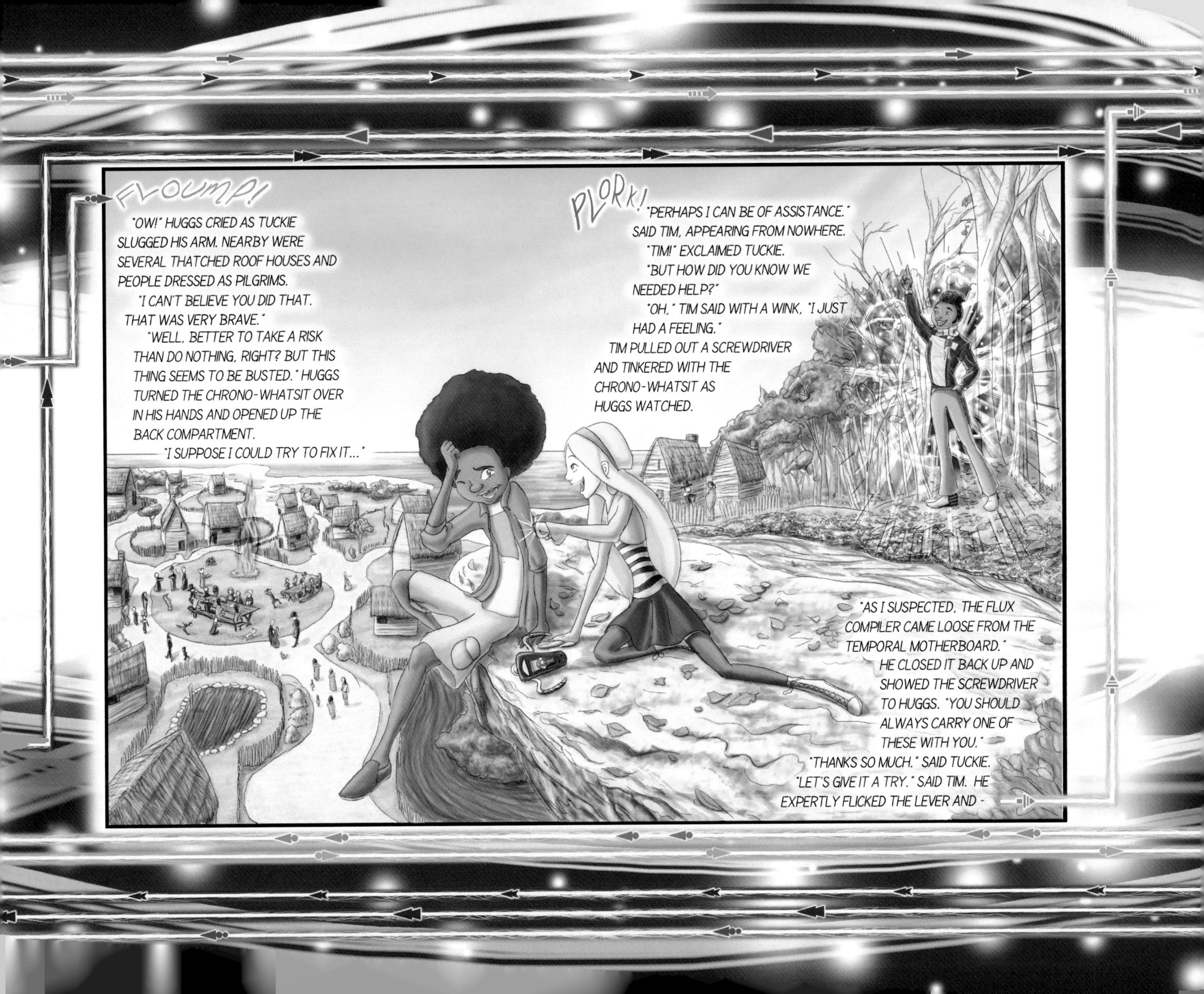
FLOUMP!
PLORK!

"OW!" HUGGS CRIED AS TUCKIE SLUGGED HIS ARM. NEARBY WERE SEVERAL THATCHED ROOF HOUSES AND PEOPLE DRESSED AS PILGRIMS.

"I CAN'T BELIEVE YOU DID THAT. THAT WAS VERY BRAVE."

"WELL, BETTER TO TAKE A RISK THAN DO NOTHING, RIGHT? BUT THIS THING SEEMS TO BE BUSTED." HUGGS TURNED THE CHRONO-WHATSIT OVER IN HIS HANDS AND OPENED UP THE BACK COMPARTMENT.

"I SUPPOSE I COULD TRY TO FIX IT..."

"PERHAPS I CAN BE OF ASSISTANCE." SAID TIM, APPEARING FROM NOWHERE.

"TIM!" EXCLAIMED TUCKIE.

"BUT HOW DID YOU KNOW WE NEEDED HELP?"

"OH," TIM SAID WITH A WINK, "I JUST HAD A FEELING."

TIM PULLED OUT A SCREWDRIVER AND TINKERED WITH THE CHRONO-WHATSIT AS HUGGS WATCHED.

"AS I SUSPECTED, THE FLUX COMPILER CAME LOOSE FROM THE TEMPORAL MOTHERBOARD."

HE CLOSED IT BACK UP AND SHOWED THE SCREWDRIVER TO HUGGS. "YOU SHOULD ALWAYS CARRY ONE OF THESE WITH YOU."

"THANKS SO MUCH." SAID TUCKIE.

"LET'S GIVE IT A TRY." SAID TIM. HE EXPERTLY FLICKED THE LEVER AND -

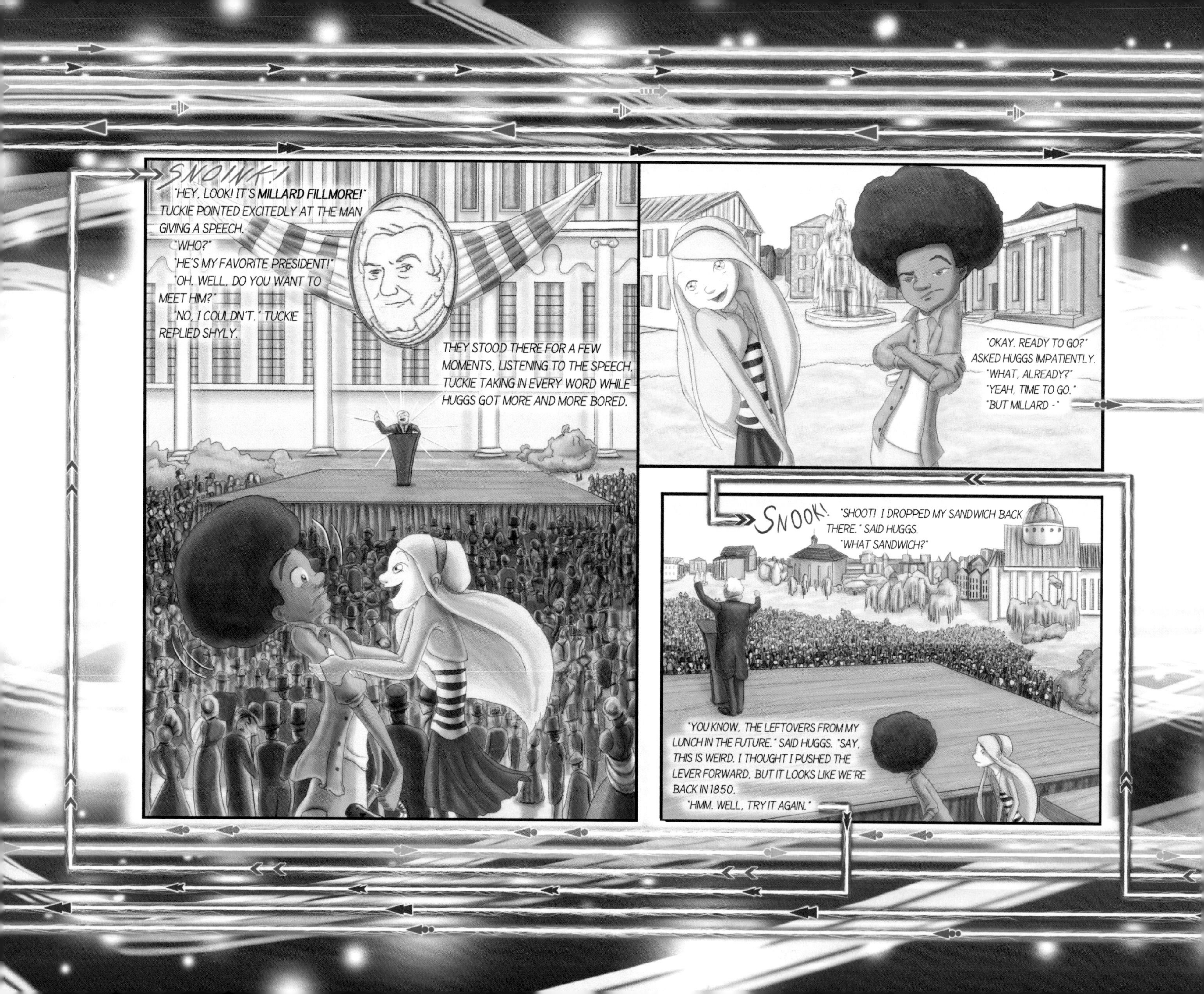
SNOINK!
"HEY, LOOK! IT'S **MILLARD FILLMORE!**" TUCKIE POINTED EXCITEDLY AT THE MAN GIVING A SPEECH.
"WHO?"
"HE'S MY FAVORITE PRESIDENT!"
"OH. WELL, DO YOU WANT TO MEET HIM?"
"NO, I COULDN'T." TUCKIE REPLIED SHYLY.
THEY STOOD THERE FOR A FEW MOMENTS, LISTENING TO THE SPEECH, TUCKIE TAKING IN EVERY WORD WHILE HUGGS GOT MORE AND MORE BORED.
"OKAY. READY TO GO?" ASKED HUGGS IMPATIENTLY.
"WHAT, ALREADY?"
"YEAH, TIME TO GO."
"BUT MILLARD -"
SNOOK!
"SHOOT! I DROPPED MY SANDWICH BACK THERE." SAID HUGGS.
"WHAT SANDWICH?"
"YOU KNOW, THE LEFTOVERS FROM MY LUNCH IN THE FUTURE." SAID HUGGS. "SAY, THIS IS WEIRD. I THOUGHT I PUSHED THE LEVER FORWARD, BUT IT LOOKS LIKE WE'RE BACK IN 1850.
"HMM. WELL, TRY IT AGAIN."

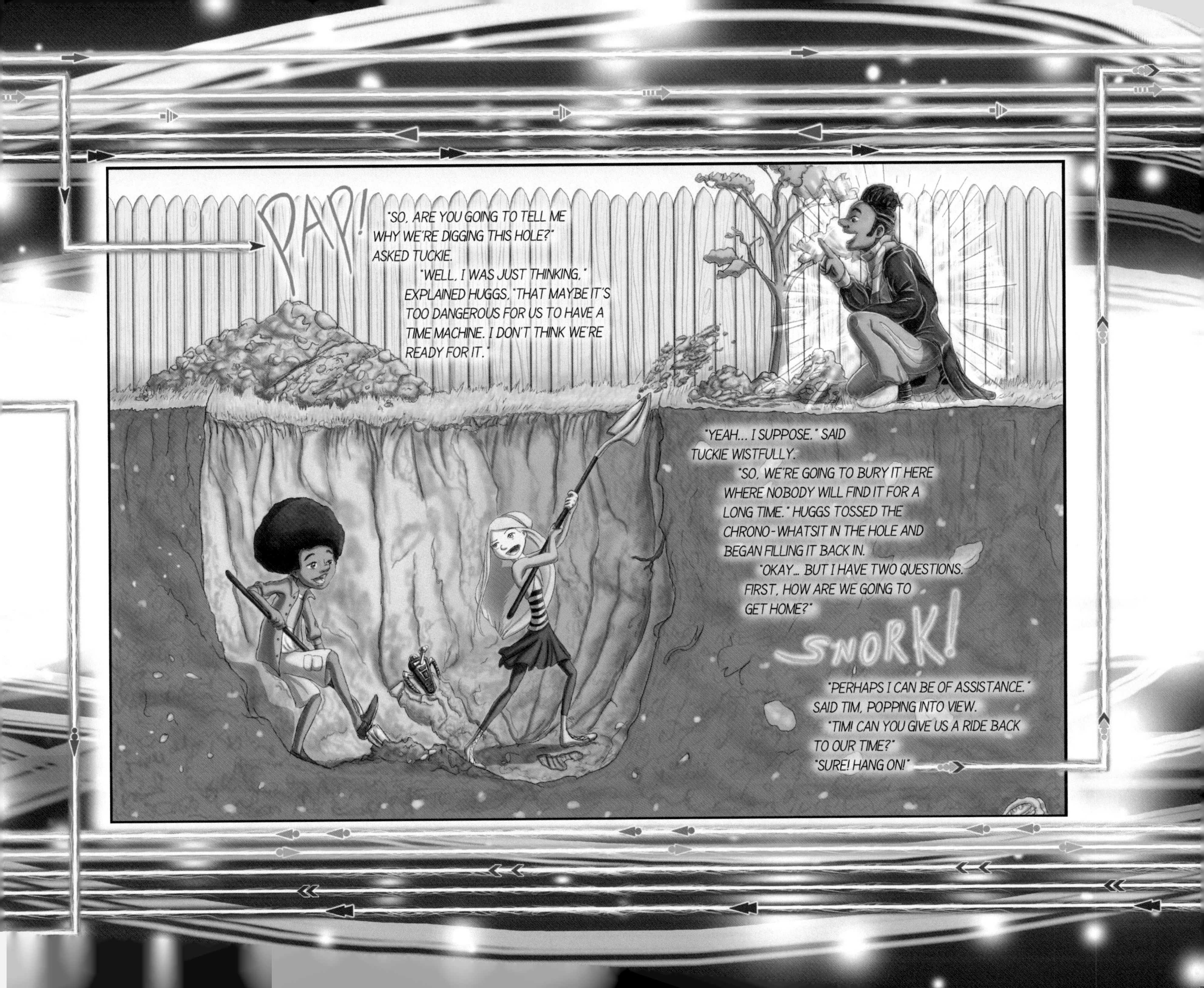
PAP!
SNORK!

"SO, ARE YOU GOING TO TELL ME WHY WE'RE DIGGING THIS HOLE?" ASKED TUCKIE.

"WELL, I WAS JUST THINKING," EXPLAINED HUGGS, "THAT MAYBE IT'S TOO DANGEROUS FOR US TO HAVE A TIME MACHINE. I DON'T THINK WE'RE READY FOR IT."

"YEAH... I SUPPOSE." SAID TUCKIE WISTFULLY.

"SO, WE'RE GOING TO BURY IT HERE WHERE NOBODY WILL FIND IT FOR A LONG TIME." HUGGS TOSSED THE CHRONO-WHATSIT IN THE HOLE AND BEGAN FILLING IT BACK IN.

"OKAY... BUT I HAVE TWO QUESTIONS. FIRST, HOW ARE WE GOING TO GET HOME?"

"PERHAPS I CAN BE OF ASSISTANCE." SAID TIM, POPPING INTO VIEW.

"TIM! CAN YOU GIVE US A RIDE BACK TO OUR TIME?"

"SURE! HANG ON!"

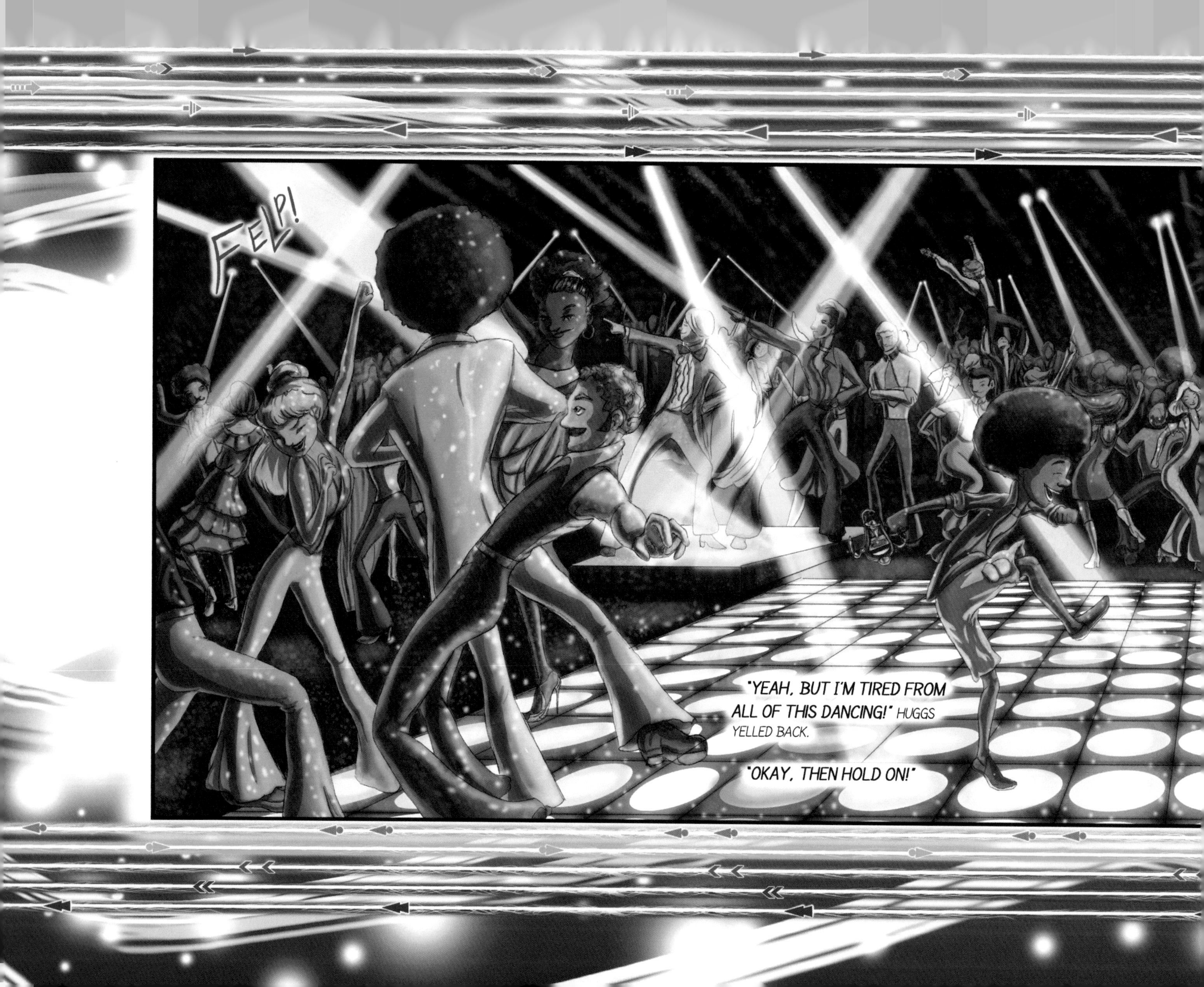
FELP!
"YEAH, BUT I'M TIRED FROM ALL OF THIS DANCING!" HUGGS YELLED BACK.
"OKAY, THEN HOLD ON!"

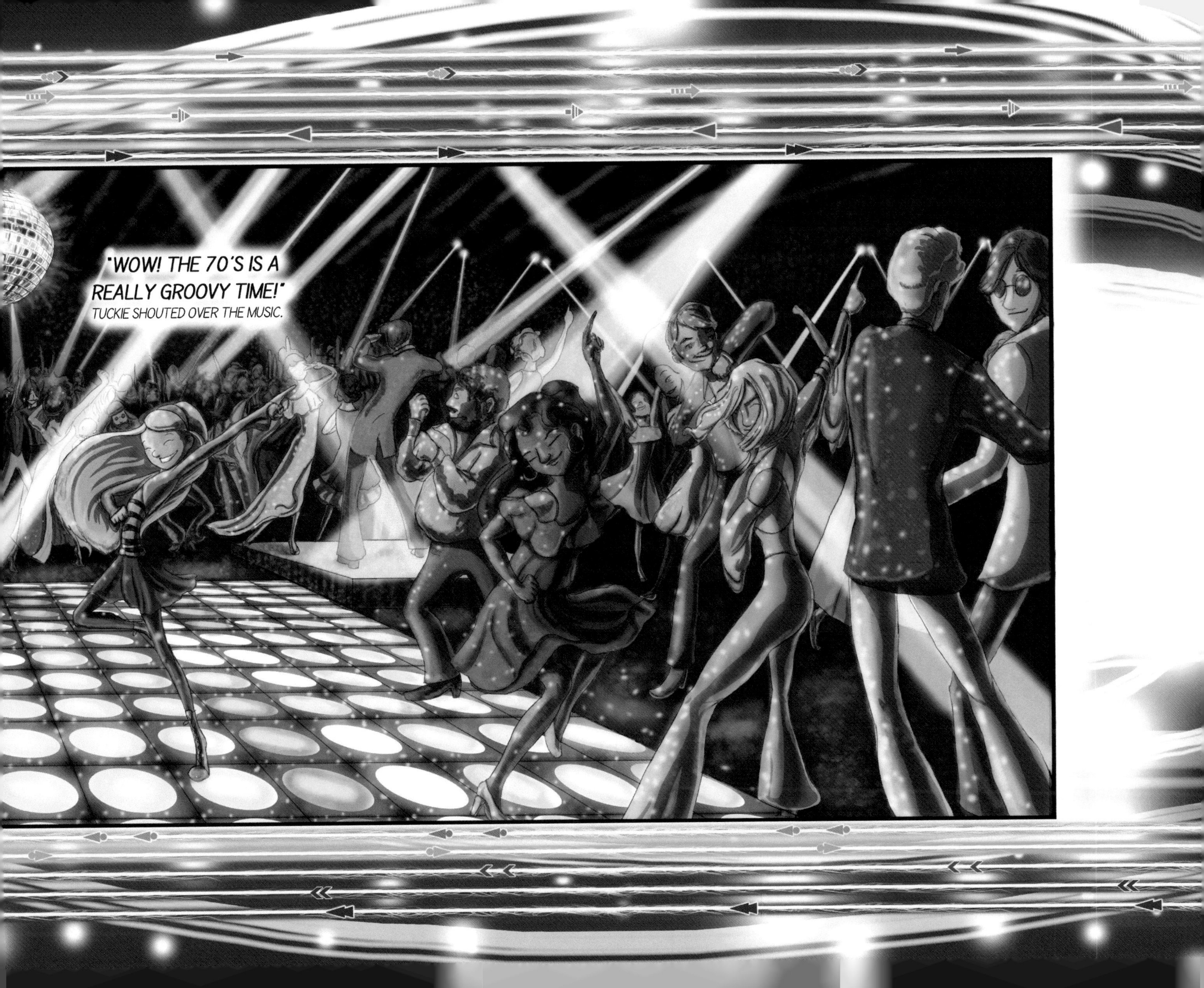
"WOW! THE 70'S IS A REALLY GROOVY TIME!"
TUCKIE SHOUTED OVER THE MUSIC.

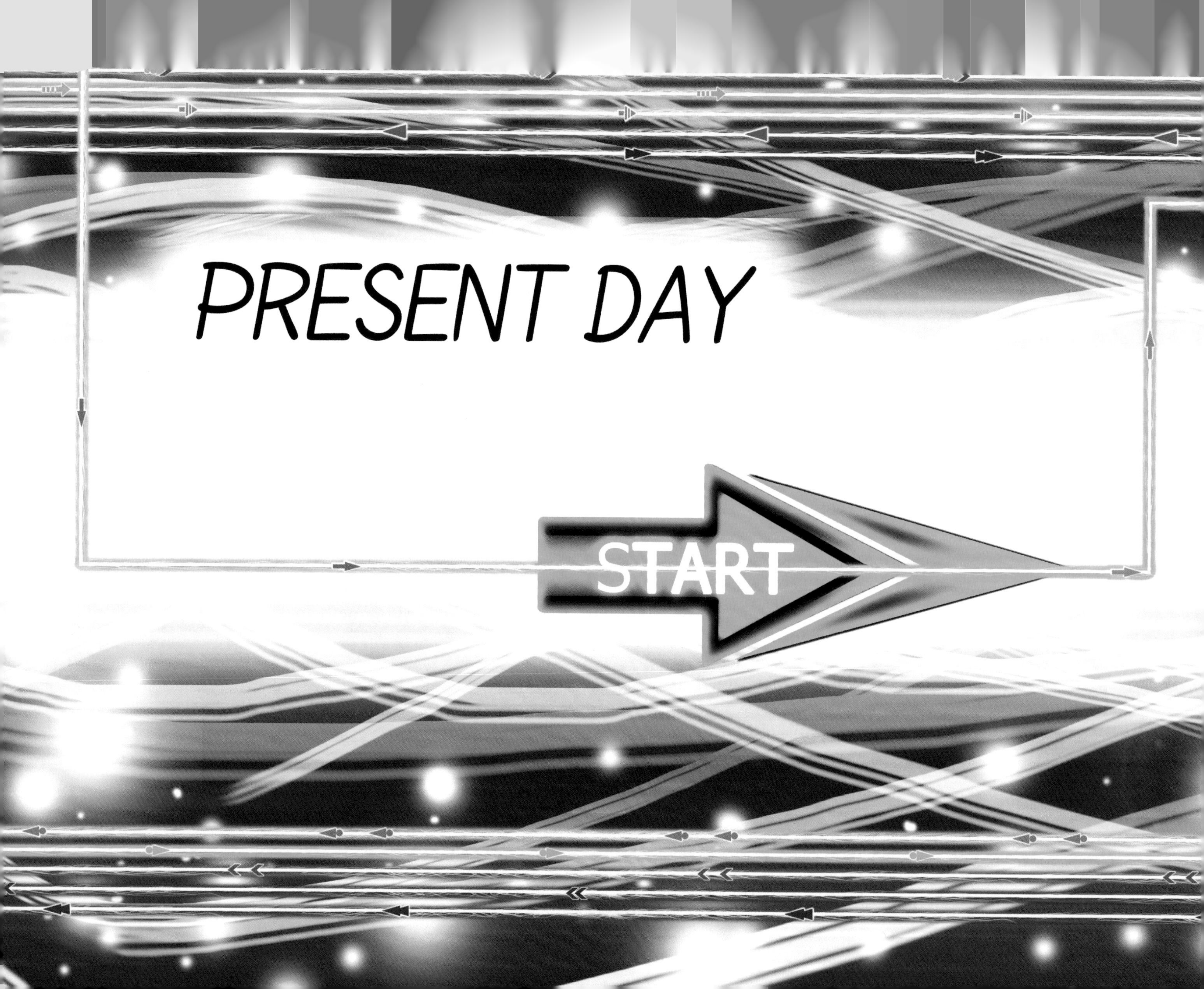
PRESENT DAY
START

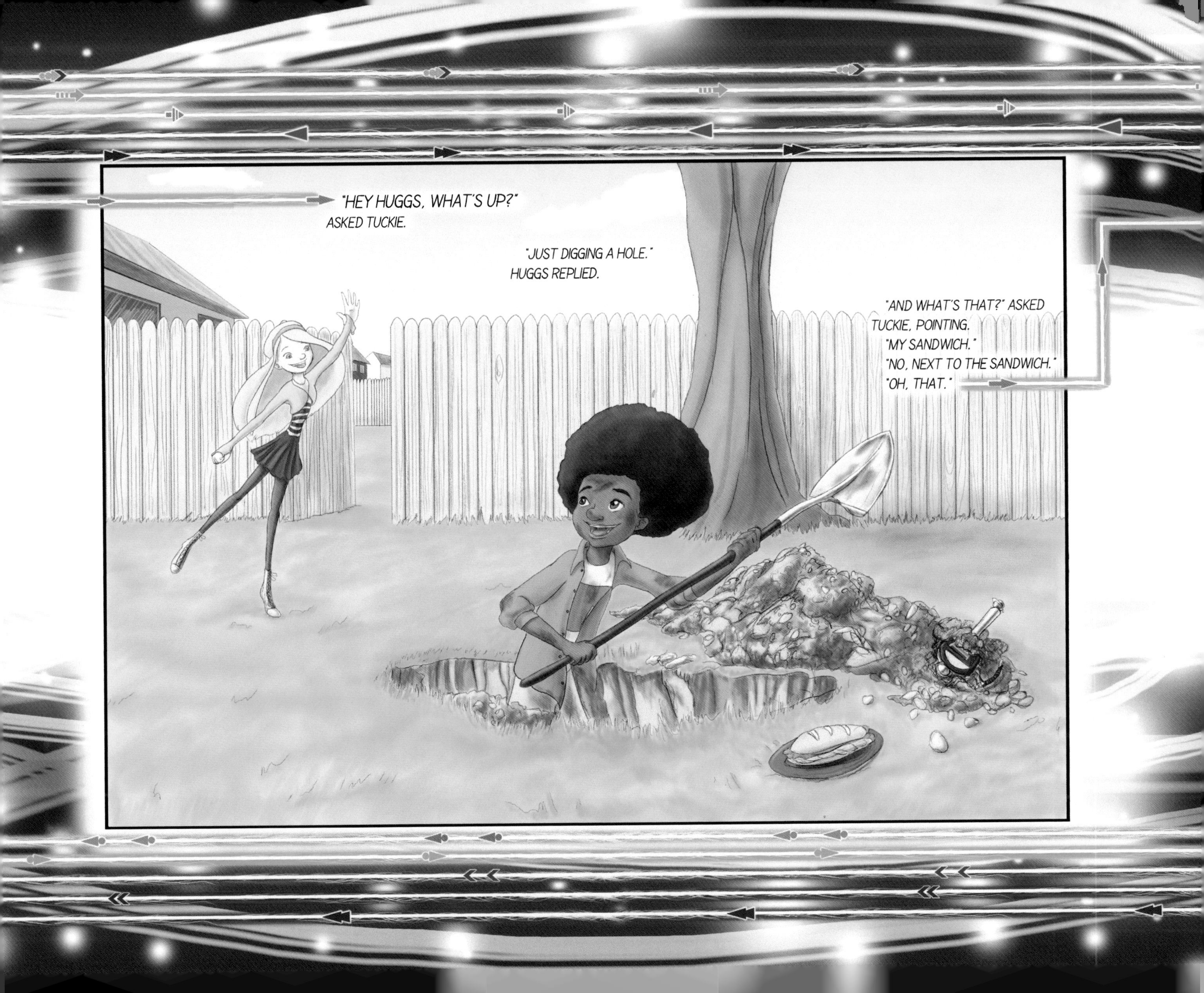
"HEY HUGGS, WHAT'S UP?"
ASKED TUCKIE.
"JUST DIGGING A HOLE."
HUGGS REPLIED.
"AND WHAT'S THAT?" ASKED
TUCKIE, POINTING.
"MY SANDWICH."
"NO, NEXT TO THE SANDWICH."
"OH, THAT."

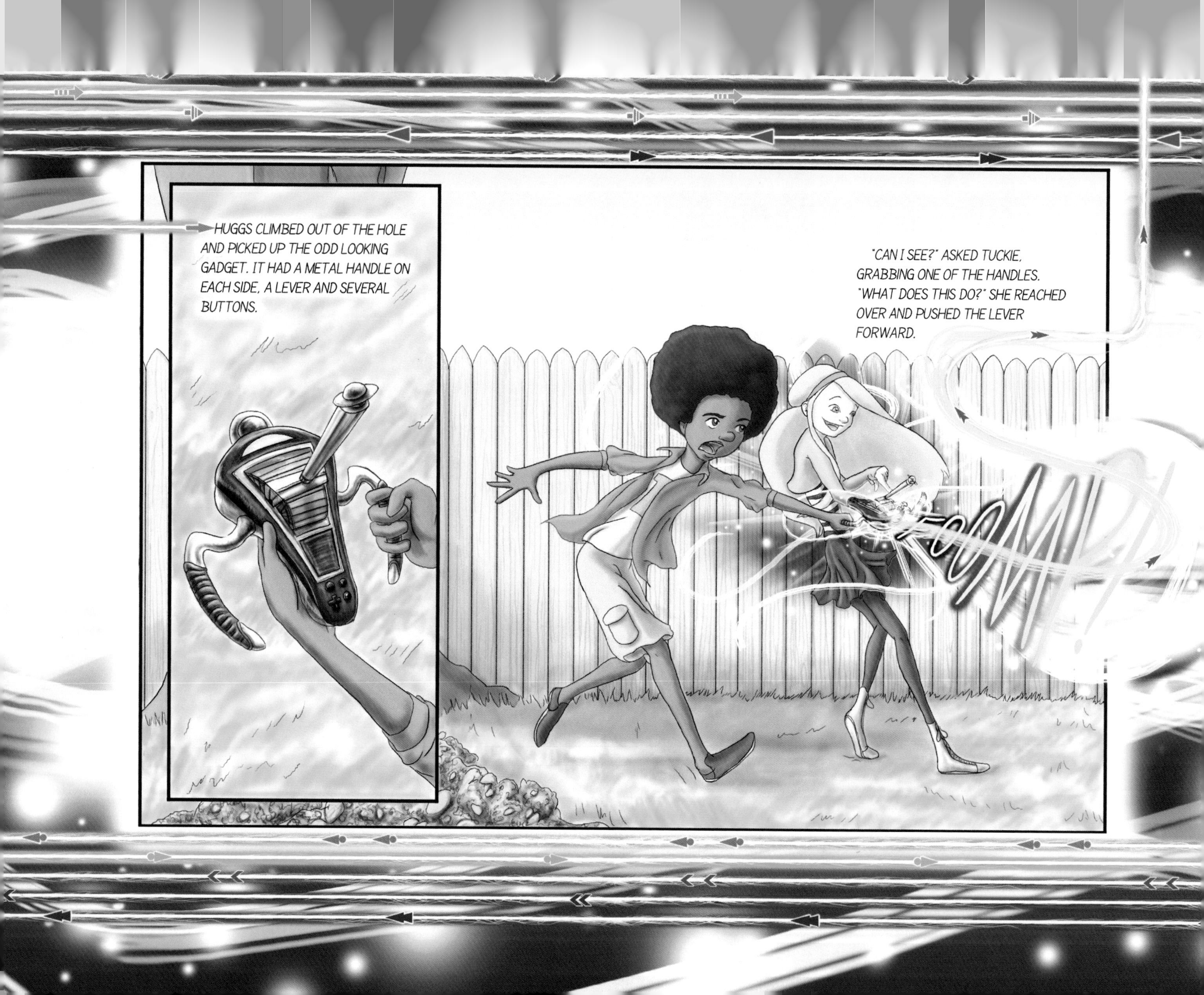
HUGGS CLIMBED OUT OF THE HOLE AND PICKED UP THE ODD LOOKING GADGET. IT HAD A METAL HANDLE ON EACH SIDE, A LEVER AND SEVERAL BUTTONS.
"CAN I SEE?" ASKED TUCKIE, GRABBING ONE OF THE HANDLES. "WHAT DOES THIS DO?" SHE REACHED OVER AND PUSHED THE LEVER FORWARD.

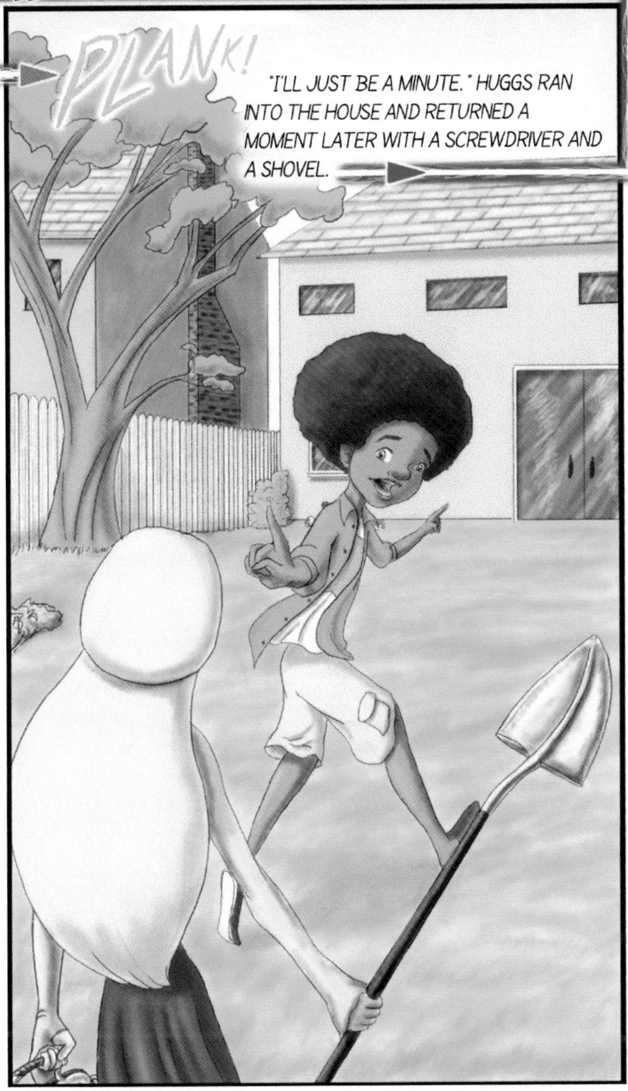
PLANK!
"I'LL JUST BE A MINUTE." HUGGS RAN INTO THE HOUSE AND RETURNED A MOMENT LATER WITH A SCREWDRIVER AND A SHOVEL.

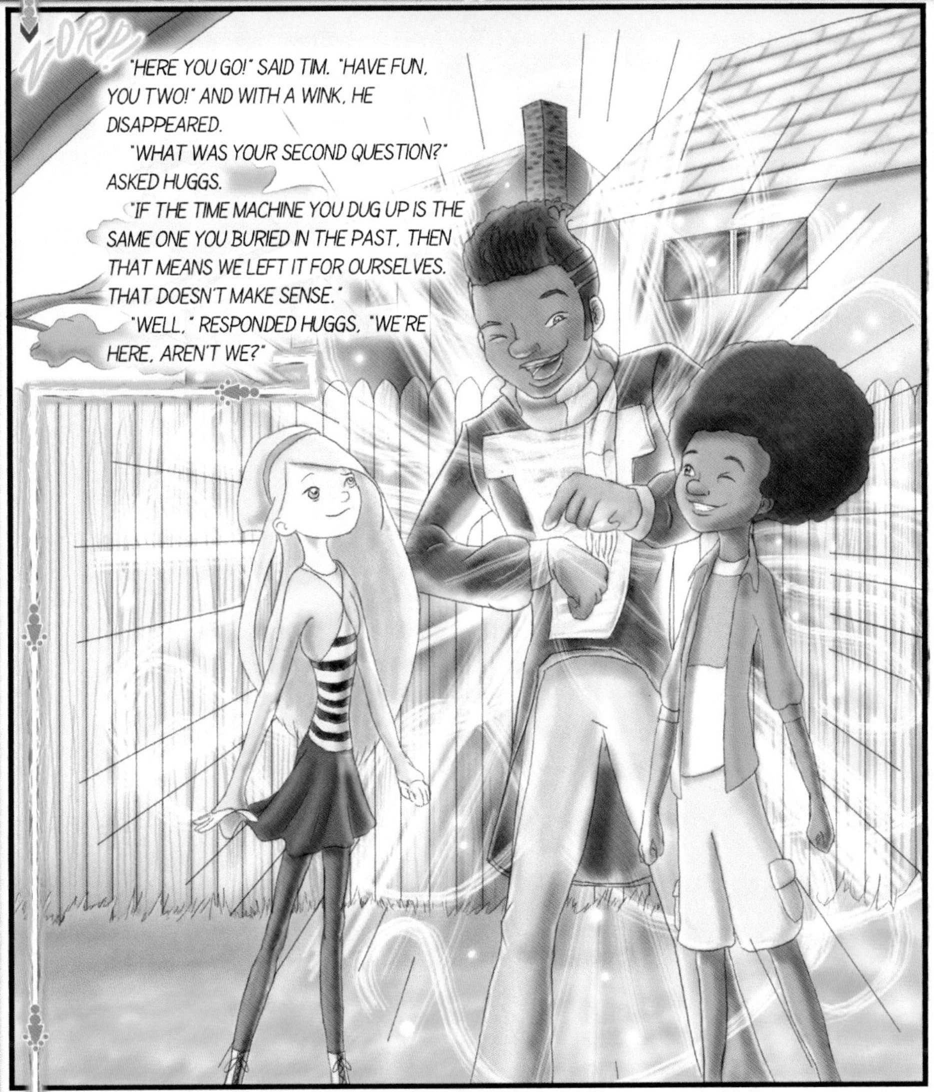
ZORP!
"HERE YOU GO!" SAID TIM. "HAVE FUN, YOU TWO!" AND WITH A WINK, HE DISAPPEARED.
"WHAT WAS YOUR SECOND QUESTION?" ASKED HUGGS.
"IF THE TIME MACHINE YOU DUG UP IS THE SAME ONE YOU BURIED IN THE PAST, THEN THAT MEANS WE LEFT IT FOR OURSELVES. THAT DOESN'T MAKE SENSE."
"WELL," RESPONDED HUGGS, "WE'RE HERE, AREN'T WE?"

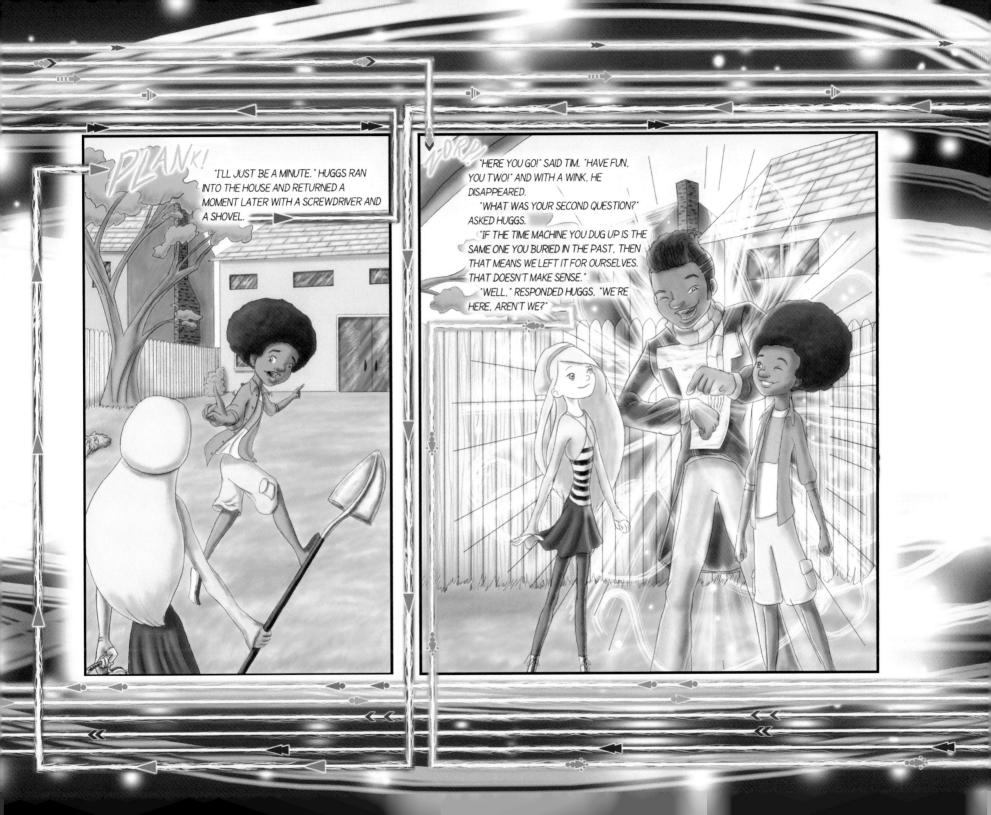

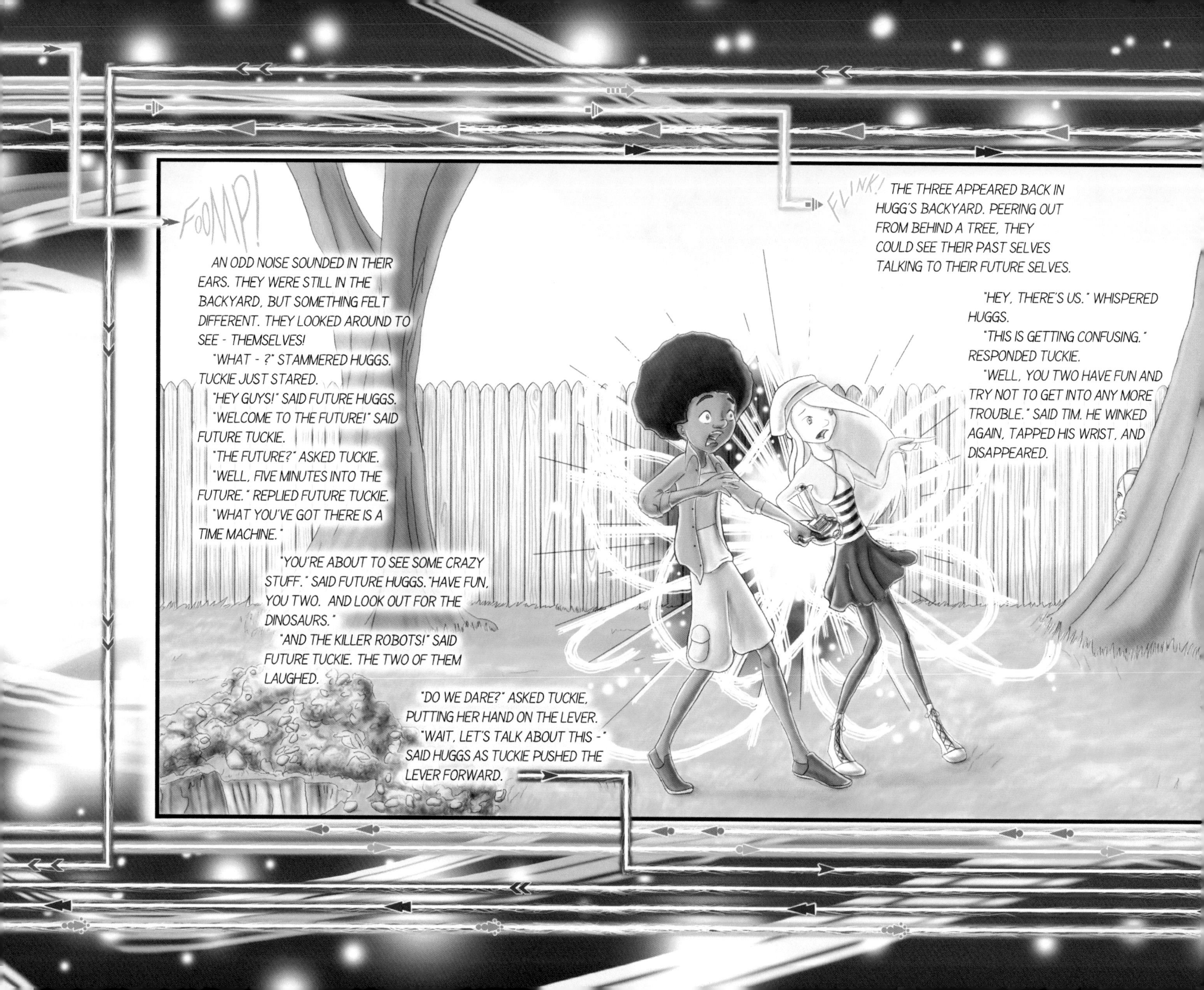
FOOMP!
FLINK!

AN ODD NOISE SOUNDED IN THEIR EARS. THEY WERE STILL IN THE BACKYARD, BUT SOMETHING FELT DIFFERENT. THEY LOOKED AROUND TO SEE - THEMSELVES!

"WHAT - ?" STAMMERED HUGGS. TUCKIE JUST STARED.

"HEY GUYS!" SAID FUTURE HUGGS.

"WELCOME TO THE FUTURE!" SAID FUTURE TUCKIE.

"THE FUTURE?" ASKED TUCKIE.

"WELL, FIVE MINUTES INTO THE FUTURE." REPLIED FUTURE TUCKIE.

"WHAT YOU'VE GOT THERE IS A TIME MACHINE."

"YOU'RE ABOUT TO SEE SOME CRAZY STUFF." SAID FUTURE HUGGS. "HAVE FUN, YOU TWO. AND LOOK OUT FOR THE DINOSAURS."

"AND THE KILLER ROBOTS!" SAID FUTURE TUCKIE. THE TWO OF THEM LAUGHED.

"DO WE DARE?" ASKED TUCKIE, PUTTING HER HAND ON THE LEVER.

"WAIT, LET'S TALK ABOUT THIS -" SAID HUGGS AS TUCKIE PUSHED THE LEVER FORWARD.

THE THREE APPEARED BACK IN HUGG'S BACKYARD. PEERING OUT FROM BEHIND A TREE, THEY COULD SEE THEIR PAST SELVES TALKING TO THEIR FUTURE SELVES.

"HEY, THERE'S US." WHISPERED HUGGS.

"THIS IS GETTING CONFUSING." RESPONDED TUCKIE.

"WELL, YOU TWO HAVE FUN AND TRY NOT TO GET INTO ANY MORE TROUBLE." SAID TIM. HE WINKED AGAIN, TAPPED HIS WRIST, AND DISAPPEARED.

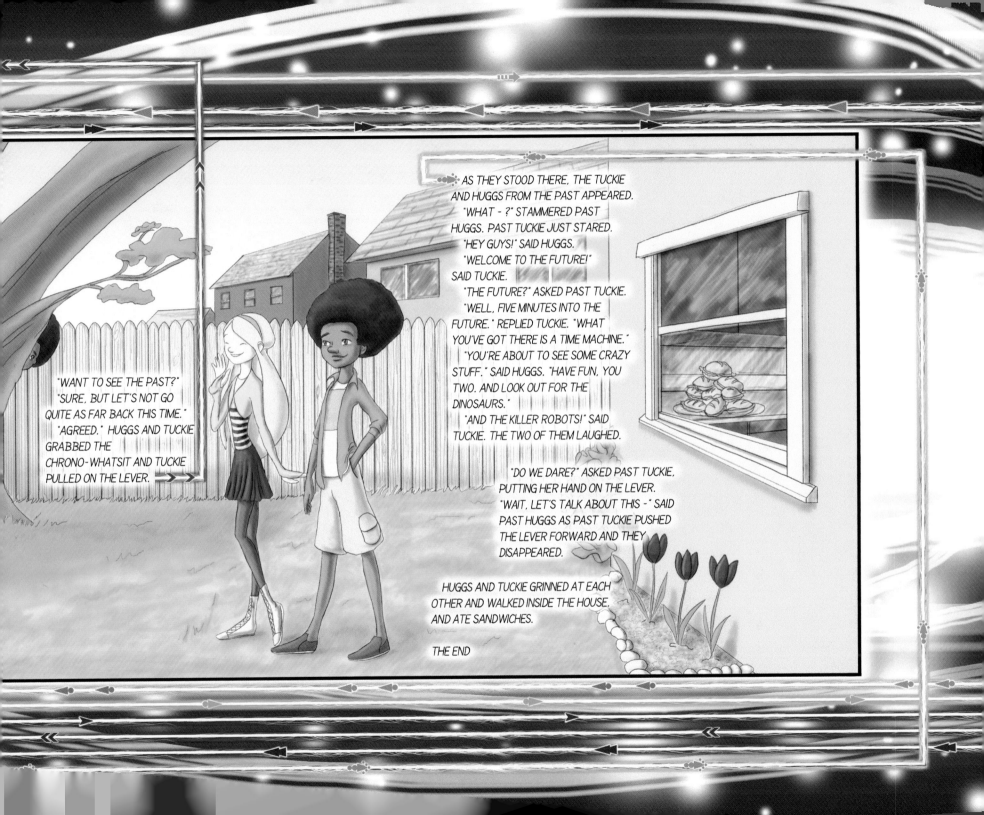

"WANT TO SEE THE PAST?"
"SURE, BUT LET'S NOT GO QUITE AS FAR BACK THIS TIME."
"AGREED." HUGGS AND TUCKIE GRABBED THE CHRONO-WHATSIT AND TUCKIE PULLED ON THE LEVER.

AS THEY STOOD THERE, THE TUCKIE AND HUGGS FROM THE PAST APPEARED.
"WHAT - ?" STAMMERED PAST HUGGS. PAST TUCKIE JUST STARED.
"HEY GUYS!" SAID HUGGS.
"WELCOME TO THE FUTURE!" SAID TUCKIE.
"THE FUTURE?" ASKED PAST TUCKIE.
"WELL, FIVE MINUTES INTO THE FUTURE." REPLIED TUCKIE. "WHAT YOU'VE GOT THERE IS A TIME MACHINE."
"YOU'RE ABOUT TO SEE SOME CRAZY STUFF." SAID HUGGS. "HAVE FUN, YOU TWO. AND LOOK OUT FOR THE DINOSAURS."
"AND THE KILLER ROBOTS!" SAID TUCKIE. THE TWO OF THEM LAUGHED.

"DO WE DARE?" ASKED PAST TUCKIE, PUTTING HER HAND ON THE LEVER.
"WAIT, LET'S TALK ABOUT THIS -" SAID PAST HUGGS AS PAST TUCKIE PUSHED THE LEVER FORWARD AND THEY DISAPPEARED.

HUGGS AND TUCKIE GRINNED AT EACH OTHER AND WALKED INSIDE THE HOUSE. AND ATE SANDWICHES.

THE END

ZOOMP!

THE TWO TIME TRAVELLERS FOUND THEMSELVES IN THE MIDDLE OF A BUSTLING CITY. ALL AROUND THEM WERE FLYING CARS AND PEOPLE WITH JETPACKS, CRAZY LOOKING SKYSCRAPERS AND PEOPLE WEARING BIZARRE CLOTHING, AND ROBOTS!

THERE WERE ROBOTS BUZZING ABOUT EVERYWHERE. HUGGS AND TUCKIE GRINNED AT EACH OTHER, THEN BEGAN LOOKING AROUND.

FOR THE NEXT FEW HOURS, THEY EXPLORED THE CITY. THEY RODE THE FUTURISTIC LOOKING BUS AND CHECKED OUT THE FUTURISTIC SHOPS AND CHECKED OUT THE STRANGE LOOKING ANIMALS IN THE FUTURISTIC PET STORE.

AFTER A WHILE, THEY STARTED TO FEEL HUNGRY, AND THEY STOPPED IN FRONT OF A RESTAURANT.

"I AM HUNGRY, BUT I DON'T KNOW IF OUR MONEY WOULD BE ANY GOOD HERE." SAID TUCKIE.

"PERHAPS I CAN BE OF ASSISTANCE." SAID A VOICE BEHIND THEM.

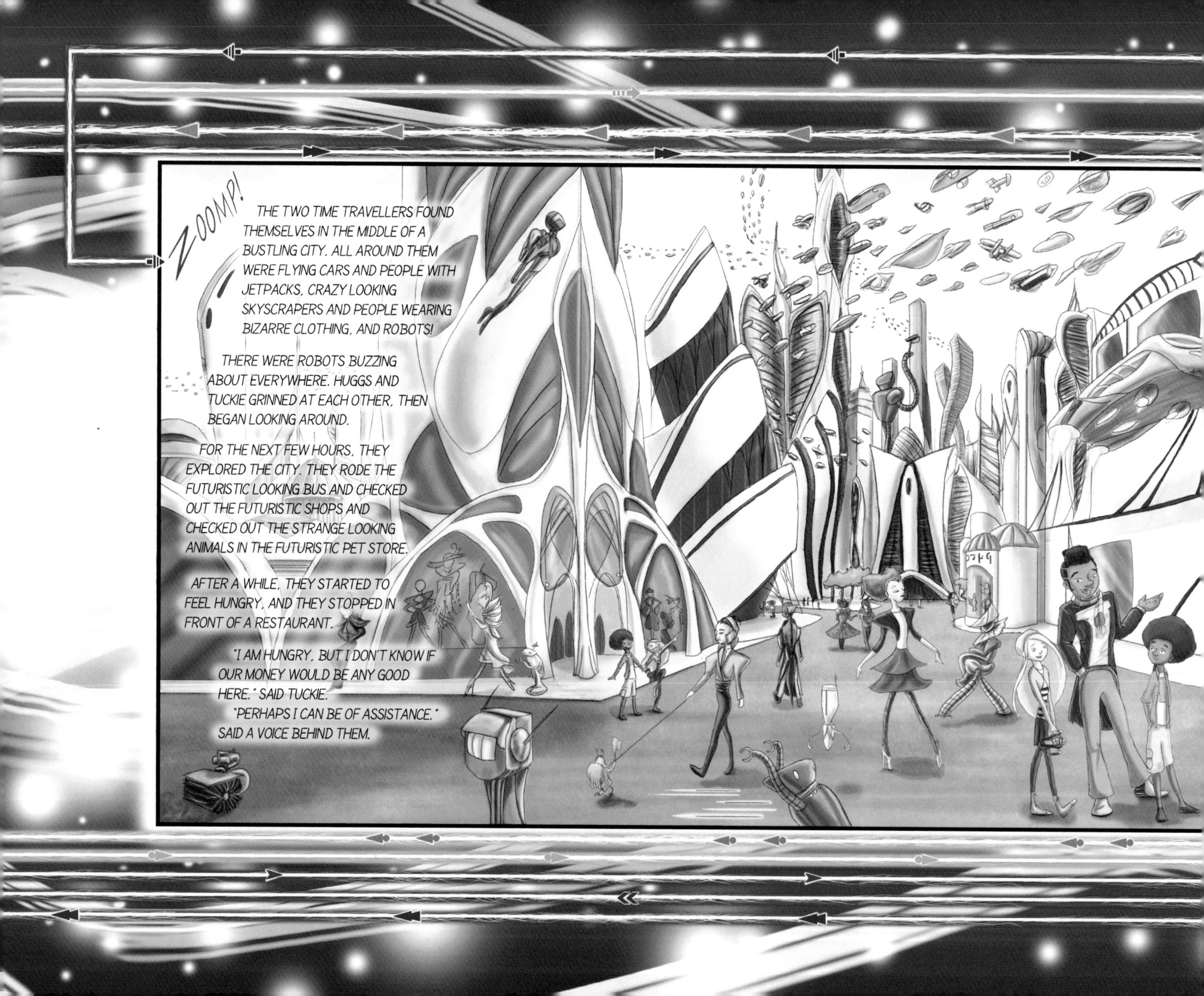

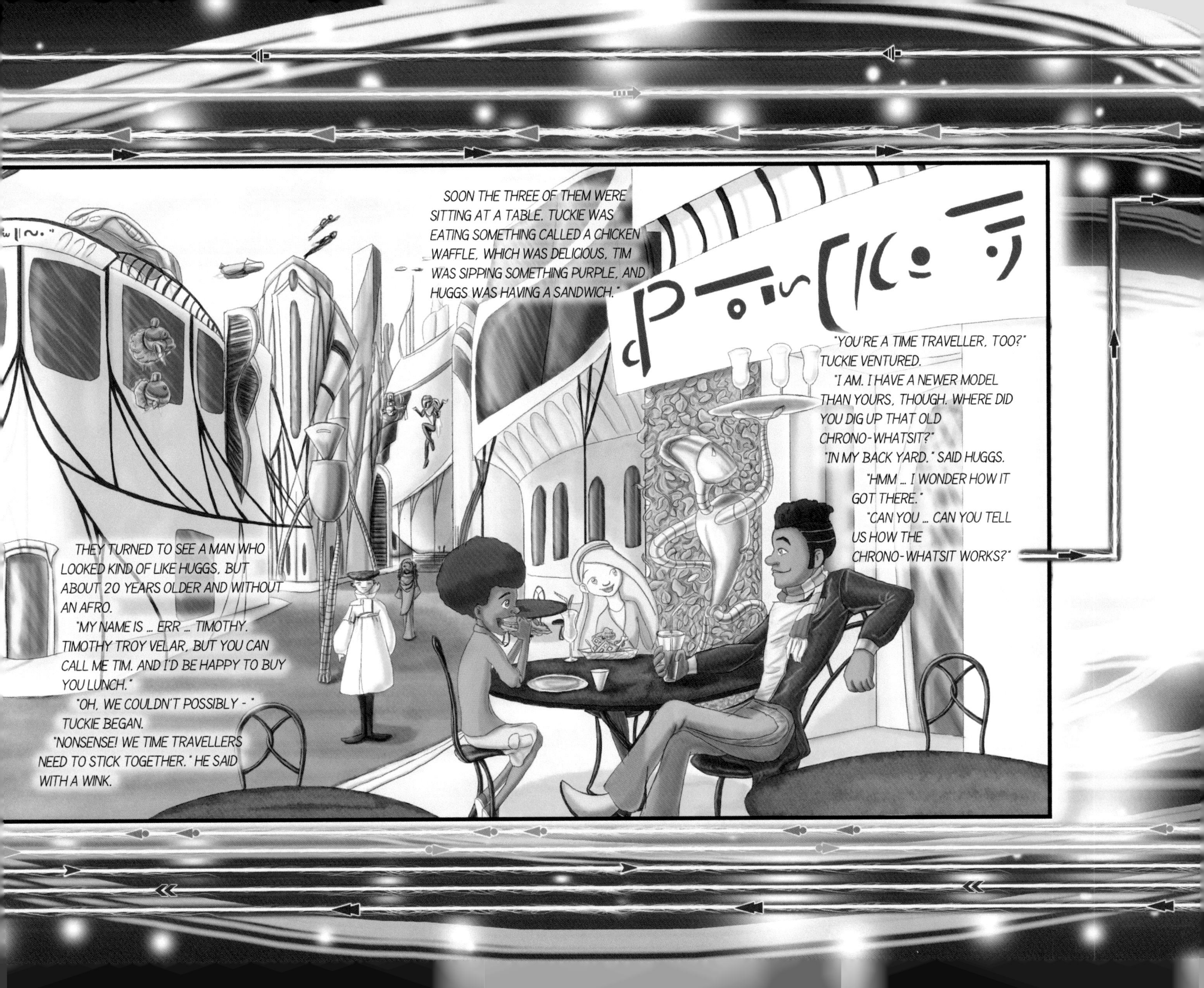

SOON THE THREE OF THEM WERE SITTING AT A TABLE. TUCKIE WAS EATING SOMETHING CALLED A CHICKEN WAFFLE, WHICH WAS DELICIOUS. TIM WAS SIPPING SOMETHING PURPLE, AND HUGGS WAS HAVING A SANDWICH."

"YOU'RE A TIME TRAVELLER, TOO?" TUCKIE VENTURED.

"I AM. I HAVE A NEWER MODEL THAN YOURS, THOUGH. WHERE DID YOU DIG UP THAT OLD CHRONO-WHATSIT?"

"IN MY BACK YARD." SAID HUGGS.

"HMM ... I WONDER HOW IT GOT THERE."

"CAN YOU ... CAN YOU TELL US HOW THE CHRONO-WHATSIT WORKS?"

THEY TURNED TO SEE A MAN WHO LOOKED KIND OF LIKE HUGGS, BUT ABOUT 20 YEARS OLDER AND WITHOUT AN AFRO.

"MY NAME IS ... ERR ... TIMOTHY. TIMOTHY TROY VELAR, BUT YOU CAN CALL ME TIM. AND I'D BE HAPPY TO BUY YOU LUNCH."

"OH, WE COULDN'T POSSIBLY - " TUCKIE BEGAN.

"NONSENSE! WE TIME TRAVELLERS NEED TO STICK TOGETHER." HE SAID WITH A WINK.

"WELL. IMAGINE A SANDWICH. A REALLY GREAT SANDWICH.

YOU'VE GOT SOME HAM,

SOME TURKEY,

SOME BACON,

THEN SOME LETTUCE,

SOME SWISS CHEESE,

THEN SOME SALAMI,

AND SO ON.

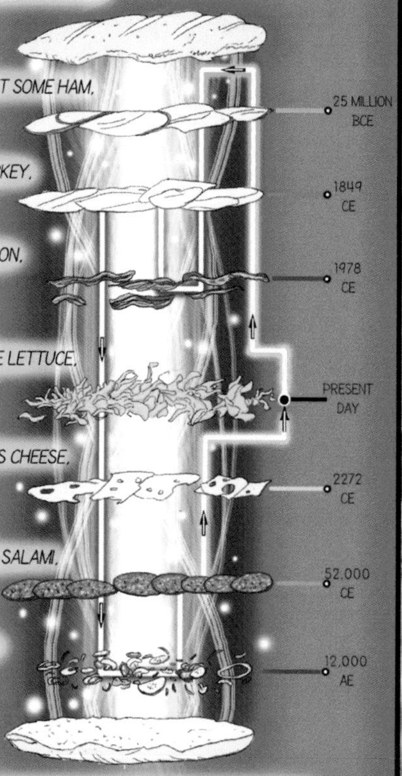

25 MILLION BCE
1849 CE
1978 CE
PRESENT DAY
2272 CE
52,000 CE
12,000 AE

AT EACH END YOU'VE GOT THE BREAD, WHICH IS SOFT AND SQUISHY, UNLESS IT'S TOASTED.

WHAT THE MACHINE DOES IS ALLOW YOU TO MOVE UP AND DOWN, FROM LAYER TO LAYER. SEE?"

"THAT DIDN'T EXPLAIN ANYTHING." TUCKIE SAID WITH A STONE FACE.

"I TOTALLY GET IT NOW!" EXCLAIMED HUGGS.

"WELL, I HAVE TO BE GOING." SAID TIM.

"THANKS FOR LUNCH." SAID TUCKIE.

"IT WAS MY PLEASURE. YOU TWO HAVE FUN." TIM TURNED AND DISAPPEARED INTO THE CROWD.

"WELL, HE CERTAINLY WAS NICE." SAID HUGGS.

"HE WAS," TUCKIE AGREED, "...BUT DID HE REMIND YOU OF ANYONE?"

"NOT REALLY." SAID HUGGS.

"SO WHERE DO YOU WANT TO GO NOW? FURTHER FORWARD?"

"OKAY!"

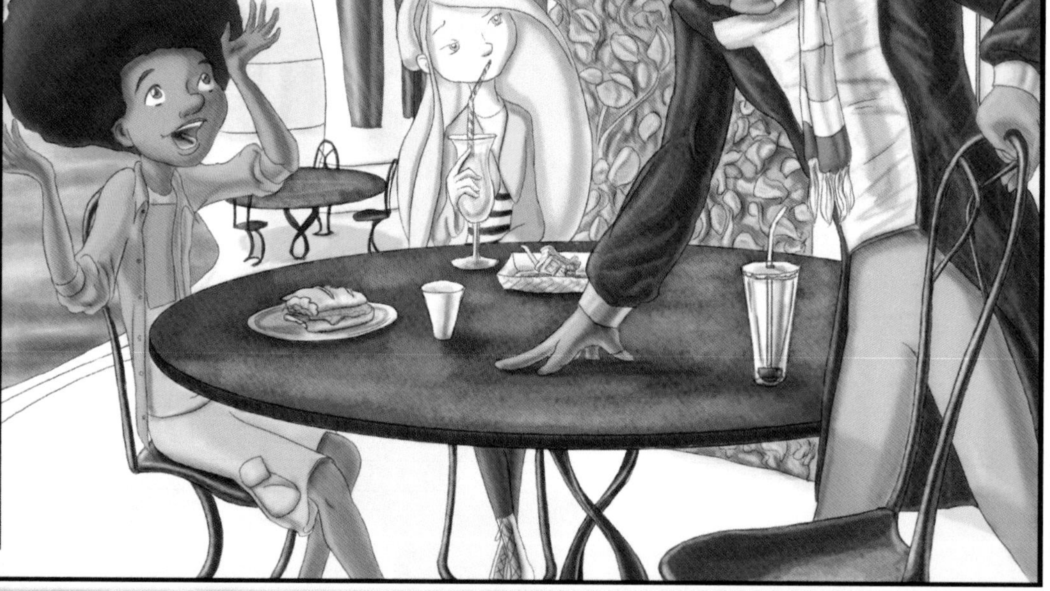

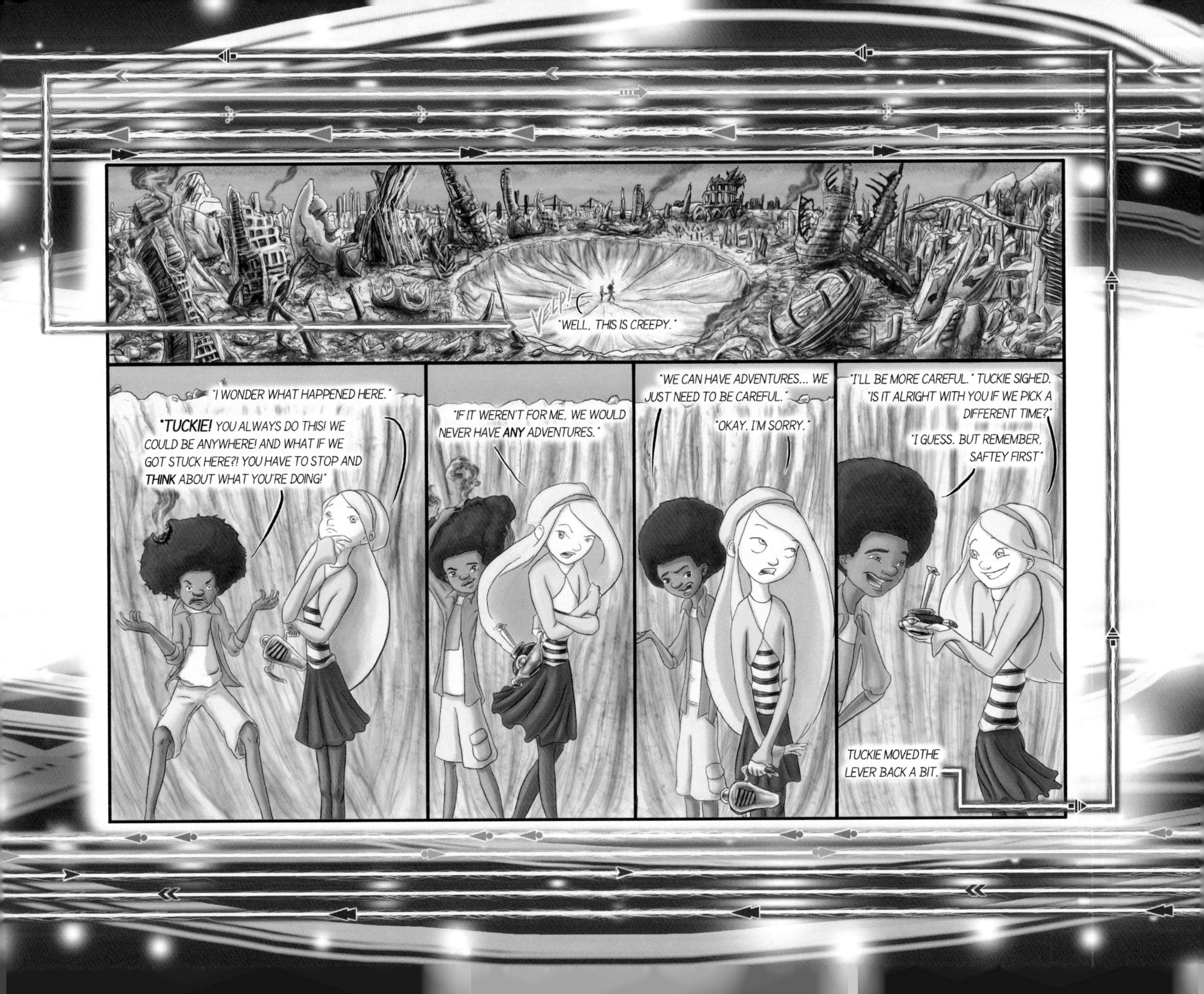
YELP!
"WELL, THIS IS CREEPY."
"I WONDER WHAT HAPPENED HERE."
"TUCKIE! YOU ALWAYS DO THIS! WE COULD BE ANYWHERE! AND WHAT IF WE GOT STUCK HERE?! YOU HAVE TO STOP AND THINK ABOUT WHAT YOU'RE DOING!"
"IF IT WEREN'T FOR ME, WE WOULD NEVER HAVE ANY ADVENTURES."
"WE CAN HAVE ADVENTURES... WE JUST NEED TO BE CAREFUL."
"OKAY. I'M SORRY."
"I'LL BE MORE CAREFUL." TUCKIE SIGHED. "IS IT ALRIGHT WITH YOU IF WE PICK A DIFFERENT TIME?"
"I GUESS. BUT REMEMBER, SAFTEY FIRST"
TUCKIE MOVED THE LEVER BACK A BIT.

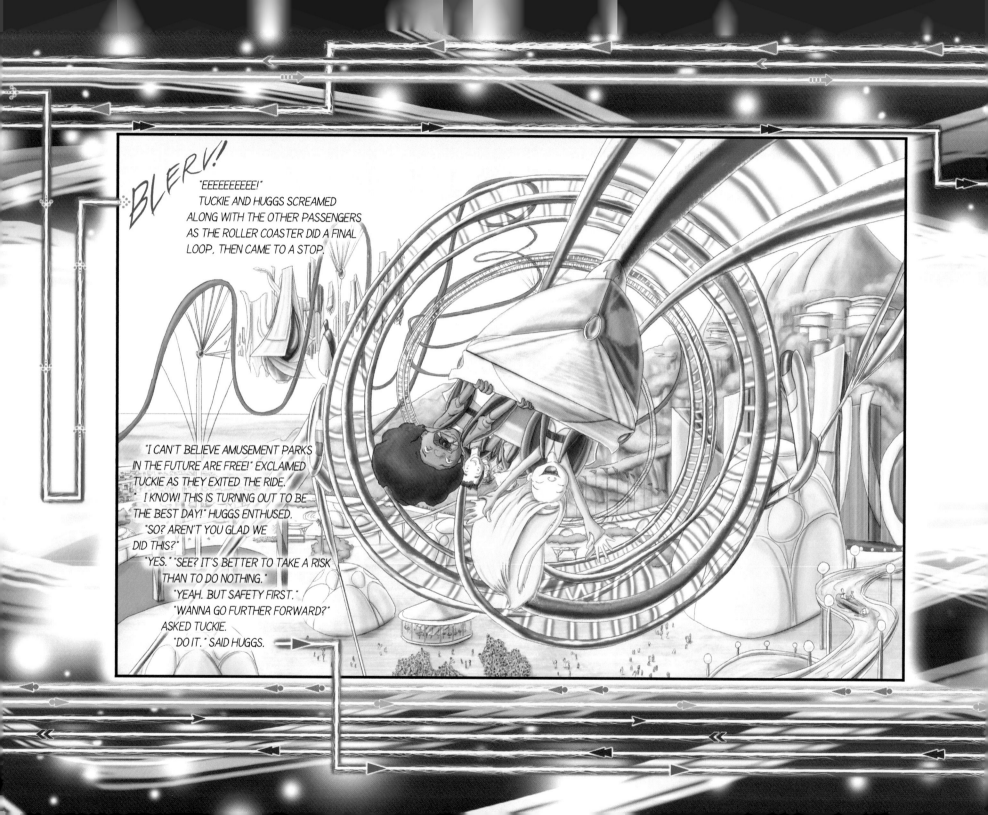

BLERV!

"EEEEEEEEEE!"
TUCKIE AND HUGGS SCREAMED
ALONG WITH THE OTHER PASSENGERS
AS THE ROLLER COASTER DID A FINAL
LOOP, THEN CAME TO A STOP.

"I CAN'T BELIEVE AMUSEMENT PARKS
IN THE FUTURE ARE FREE!" EXCLAIMED
TUCKIE AS THEY EXITED THE RIDE.
"I KNOW! THIS IS TURNING OUT TO BE
THE BEST DAY!" HUGGS ENTHUSED.
"SO? AREN'T YOU GLAD WE
DID THIS?"
"YES." "SEE? IT'S BETTER TO TAKE A RISK
THAN TO DO NOTHING."
"YEAH. BUT SAFETY FIRST."
"WANNA GO FURTHER FORWARD?"
ASKED TUCKIE.
"DO IT." SAID HUGGS.

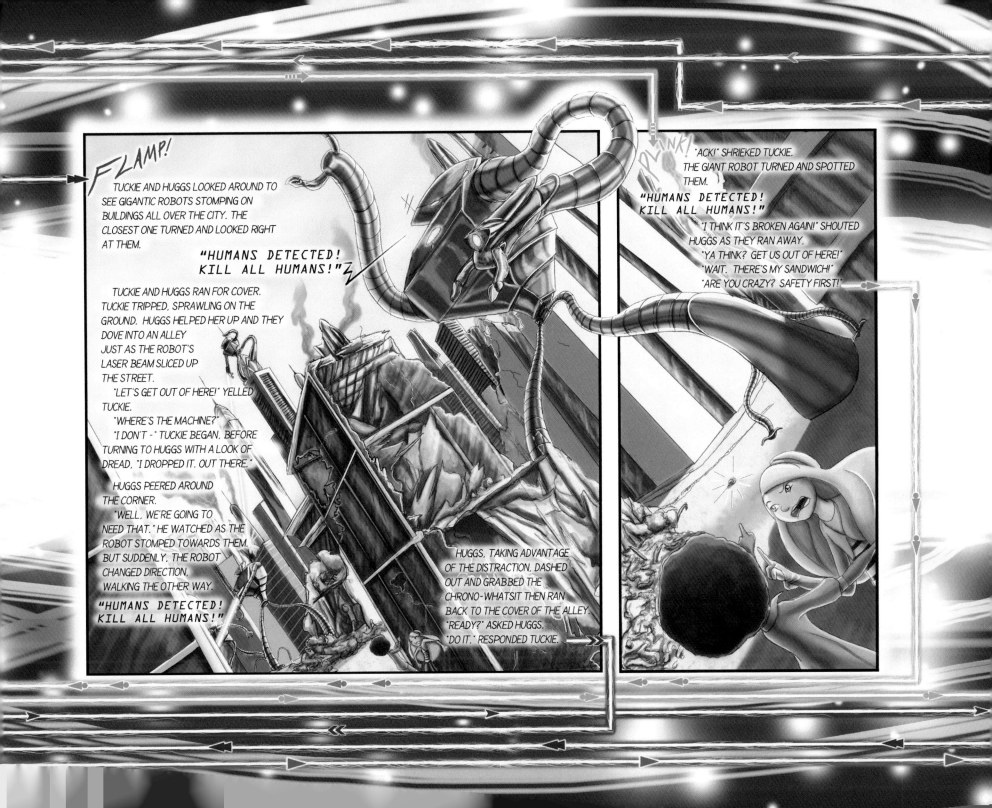

FLAMP!

TUCKIE AND HUGGS LOOKED AROUND TO SEE GIGANTIC ROBOTS STOMPING ON BUILDINGS ALL OVER THE CITY. THE CLOSEST ONE TURNED AND LOOKED RIGHT AT THEM.

"HUMANS DETECTED! KILL ALL HUMANS!"

TUCKIE AND HUGGS RAN FOR COVER. TUCKIE TRIPPED, SPRAWLING ON THE GROUND. HUGGS HELPED HER UP AND THEY DOVE INTO AN ALLEY JUST AS THE ROBOT'S LASER BEAM SLICED UP THE STREET.

"LET'S GET OUT OF HERE!" YELLED TUCKIE.

"WHERE'S THE MACHINE?"

"I DON'T -" TUCKIE BEGAN, BEFORE TURNING TO HUGGS WITH A LOOK OF DREAD, "I DROPPED IT. OUT THERE."

HUGGS PEERED AROUND THE CORNER.

"WELL, WE'RE GOING TO NEED THAT." HE WATCHED AS THE ROBOT STOMPED TOWARDS THEM. BUT SUDDENLY, THE ROBOT CHANGED DIRECTION, WALKING THE OTHER WAY.

"HUMANS DETECTED! KILL ALL HUMANS!"

HUGGS, TAKING ADVANTAGE OF THE DISTRACTION, DASHED OUT AND GRABBED THE CHRONO-WHATSIT THEN RAN BACK TO THE COVER OF THE ALLEY.

"READY?" ASKED HUGGS.

"DO IT." RESPONDED TUCKIE.

PLINK!

"ACK!" SHRIEKED TUCKIE. THE GIANT ROBOT TURNED AND SPOTTED THEM.

"HUMANS DETECTED! KILL ALL HUMANS!"

"I THINK IT'S BROKEN AGAIN!" SHOUTED HUGGS AS THEY RAN AWAY.

"YA THINK? GET US OUT OF HERE!"

"WAIT. THERE'S MY SANDWICH!"

"ARE YOU CRAZY? SAFETY FIRST!"

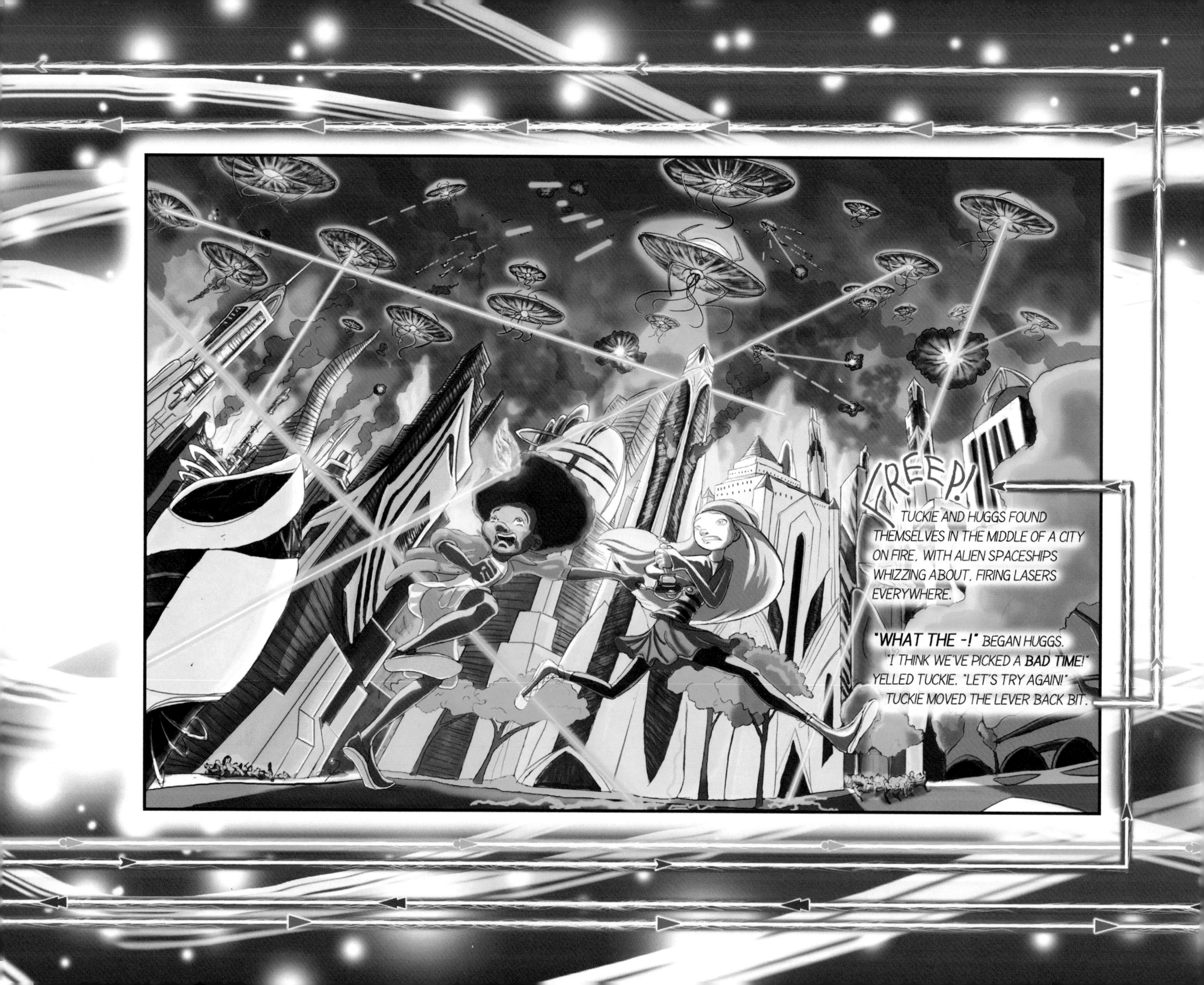
FREEP!
TUCKIE AND HUGGS FOUND THEMSELVES IN THE MIDDLE OF A CITY ON FIRE, WITH ALIEN SPACESHIPS WHIZZING ABOUT, FIRING LASERS EVERYWHERE.
"WHAT THE -!" BEGAN HUGGS.
"I THINK WE'VE PICKED A BAD TIME!" YELLED TUCKIE. "LET'S TRY AGAIN!"
TUCKIE MOVED THE LEVER BACK BIT.

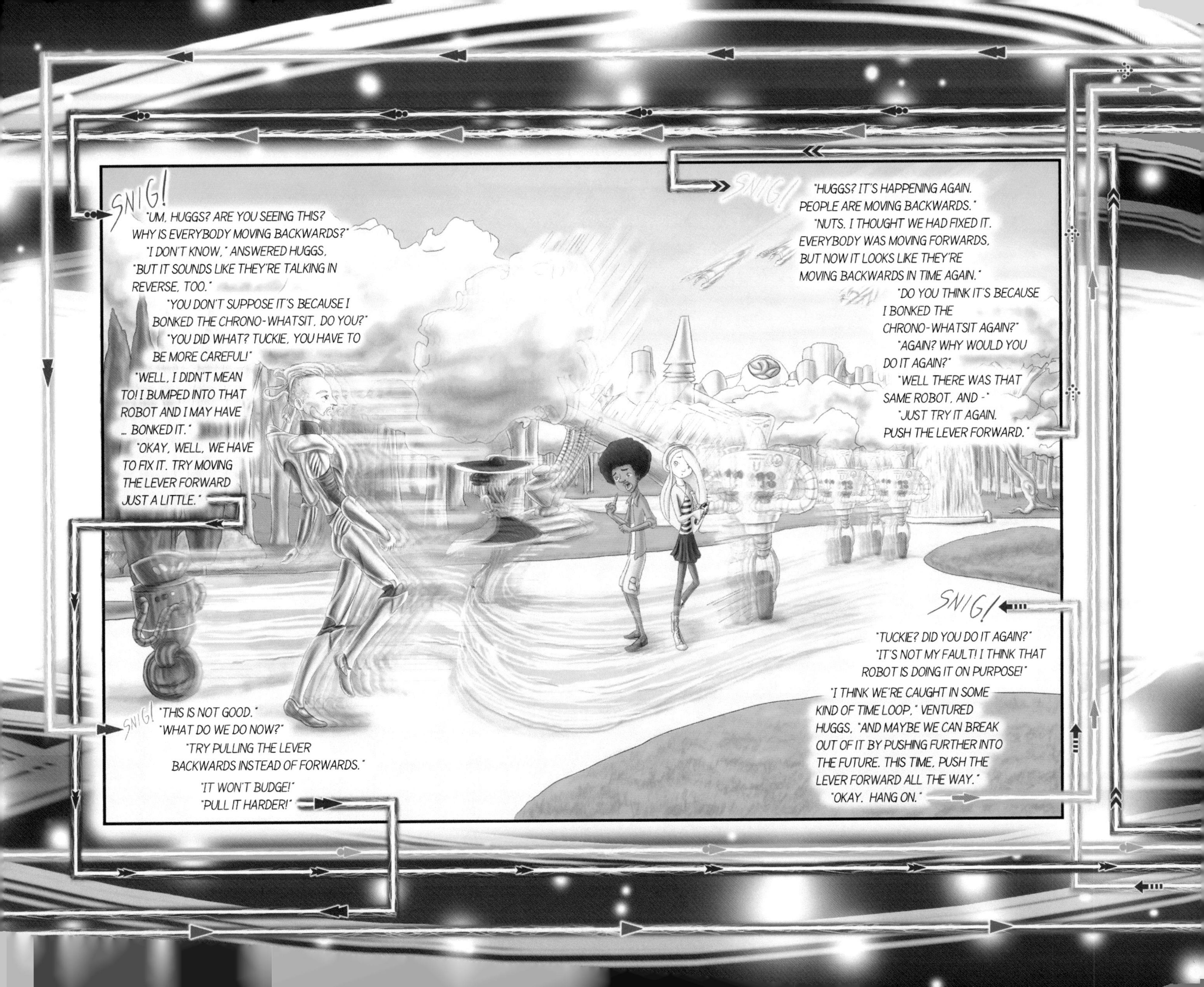

SNIG! "UM, HUGGS? ARE YOU SEEING THIS? WHY IS EVERYBODY MOVING BACKWARDS?"

"I DON'T KNOW," ANSWERED HUGGS, "BUT IT SOUNDS LIKE THEY'RE TALKING IN REVERSE, TOO."

"YOU DON'T SUPPOSE IT'S BECAUSE I BONKED THE CHRONO-WHATSIT, DO YOU?"

"YOU DID WHAT? TUCKIE, YOU HAVE TO BE MORE CAREFUL!"

"WELL, I DIDN'T MEAN TO! I BUMPED INTO THAT ROBOT AND I MAY HAVE ... BONKED IT."

"OKAY, WELL, WE HAVE TO FIX IT. TRY MOVING THE LEVER FORWARD JUST A LITTLE."

SNIG! "THIS IS NOT GOOD."

"WHAT DO WE DO NOW?"

"TRY PULLING THE LEVER BACKWARDS INSTEAD OF FORWARDS."

"IT WON'T BUDGE!"

"PULL IT HARDER!"

SNIG! "HUGGS? IT'S HAPPENING AGAIN. PEOPLE ARE MOVING BACKWARDS."

"NUTS. I THOUGHT WE HAD FIXED IT. EVERYBODY WAS MOVING FORWARDS, BUT NOW IT LOOKS LIKE THEY'RE MOVING BACKWARDS IN TIME AGAIN."

"DO YOU THINK IT'S BECAUSE I BONKED THE CHRONO-WHATSIT AGAIN?"

"AGAIN? WHY WOULD YOU DO IT AGAIN?"

"WELL THERE WAS THAT SAME ROBOT, AND -"

"JUST TRY IT AGAIN. PUSH THE LEVER FORWARD."

SNIG! "TUCKIE? DID YOU DO IT AGAIN?"

"IT'S NOT MY FAULT! I THINK THAT ROBOT IS DOING IT ON PURPOSE!"

"I THINK WE'RE CAUGHT IN SOME KIND OF TIME LOOP," VENTURED HUGGS, "AND MAYBE WE CAN BREAK OUT OF IT BY PUSHING FURTHER INTO THE FUTURE. THIS TIME, PUSH THE LEVER FORWARD ALL THE WAY."

"OKAY. HANG ON."

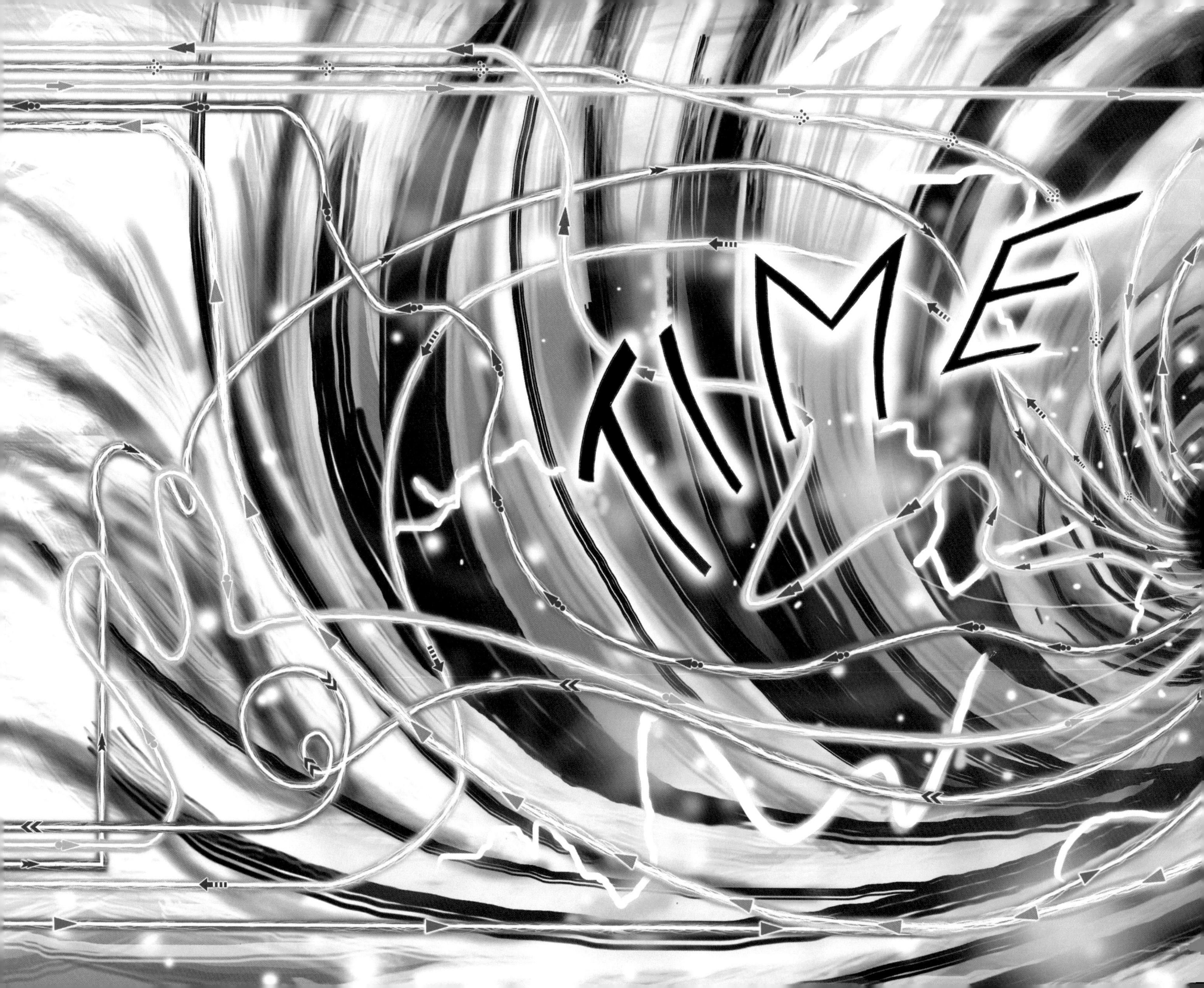
TIME

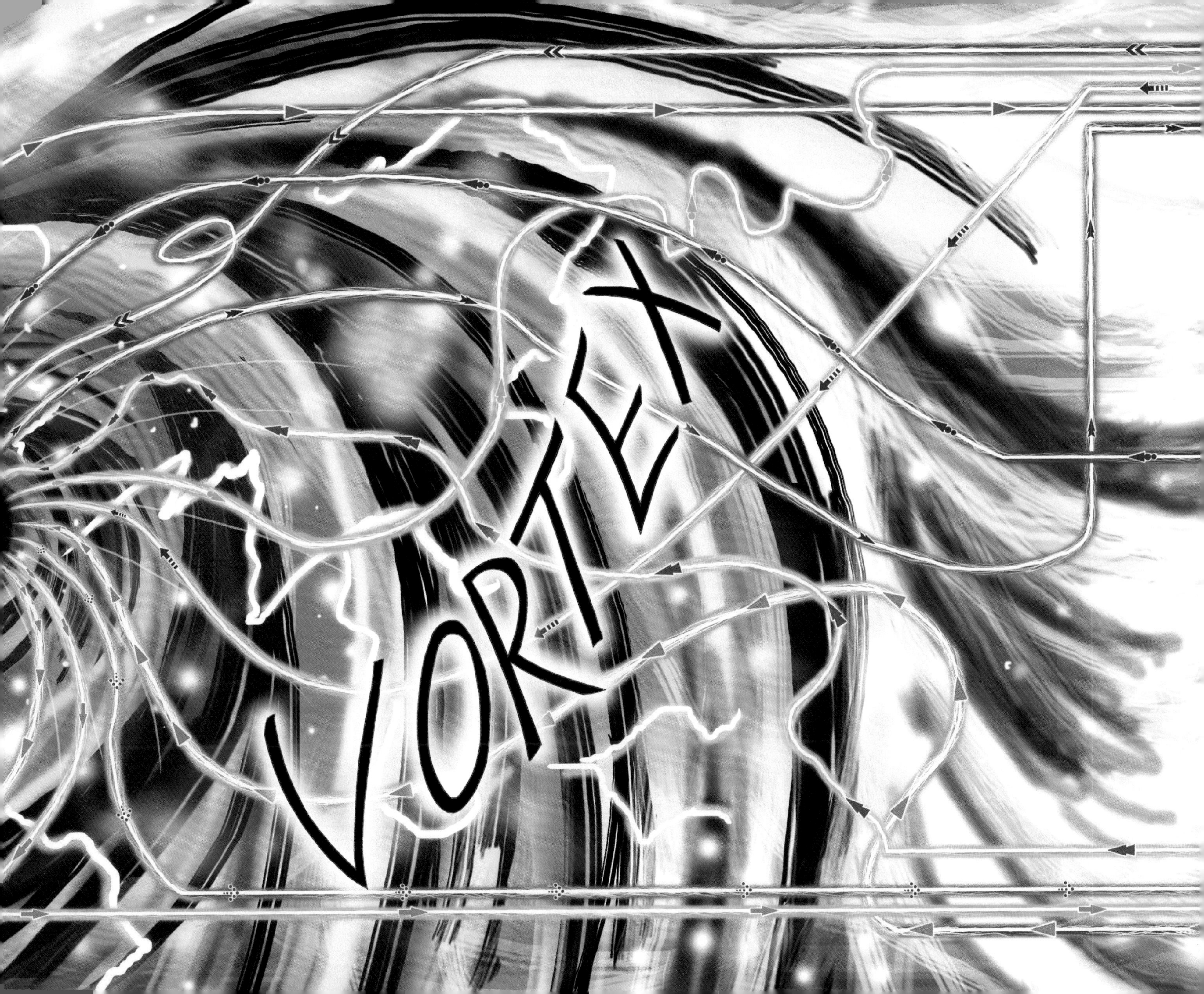
VORTEX

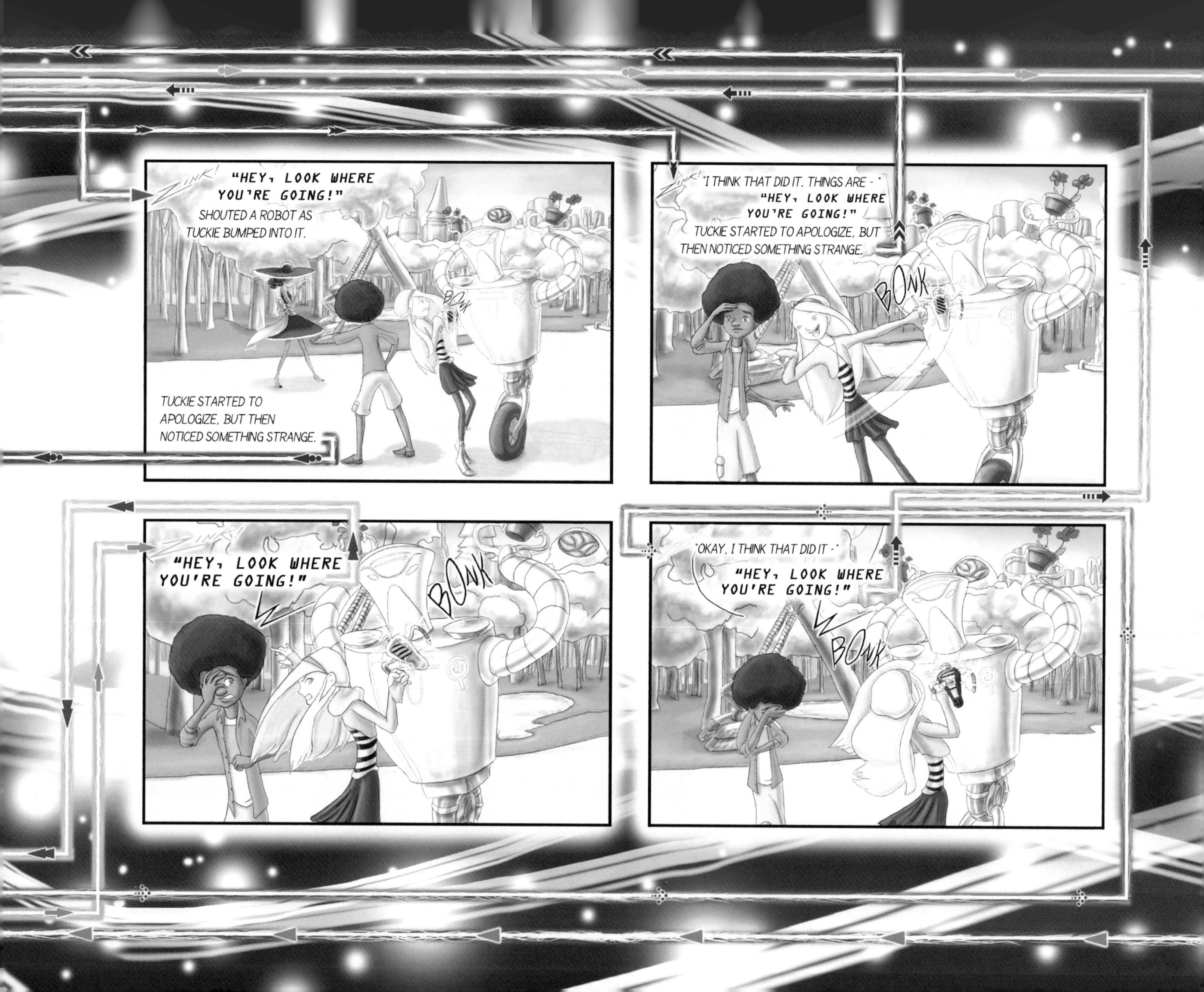
ZINK!
"HEY, LOOK WHERE YOU'RE GOING!"
SHOUTED A ROBOT AS TUCKIE BUMPED INTO IT.
BONK
TUCKIE STARTED TO APOLOGIZE, BUT THEN NOTICED SOMETHING STRANGE.
ZINK!
"I THINK THAT DID IT. THINGS ARE - "
"HEY, LOOK WHERE YOU'RE GOING!"
TUCKIE STARTED TO APOLOGIZE, BUT THEN NOTICED SOMETHING STRANGE.
BONK
ZINK!
"HEY, LOOK WHERE YOU'RE GOING!"
BONK
"OKAY, I THINK THAT DID IT -"
"HEY, LOOK WHERE YOU'RE GOING!"
BONK

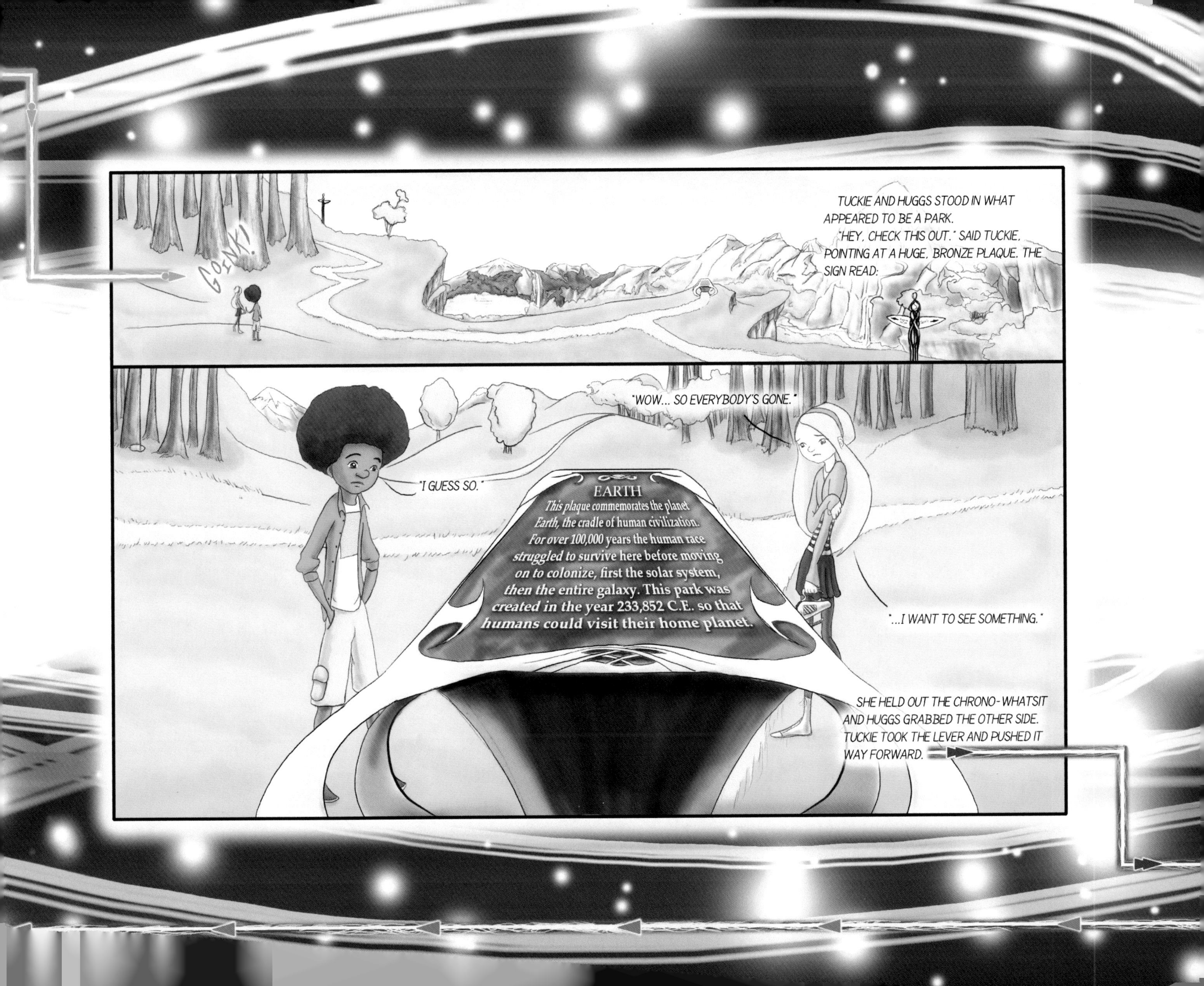
TUCKIE AND HUGGS STOOD IN WHAT APPEARED TO BE A PARK.
"HEY, CHECK THIS OUT." SAID TUCKIE, POINTING AT A HUGE, BRONZE PLAQUE. THE SIGN READ:
GOINK!
EARTH
This plaque commemorates the planet Earth, the cradle of human civilization. For over 100,000 years the human race struggled to survive here before moving on to colonize, first the solar system, then the entire galaxy. This park was created in the year 233,852 C.E. so that humans could visit their home planet.
"WOW... SO EVERYBODY'S GONE."
"I GUESS SO."
"...I WANT TO SEE SOMETHING."
SHE HELD OUT THE CHRONO-WHATSIT AND HUGGS GRABBED THE OTHER SIDE. TUCKIE TOOK THE LEVER AND PUSHED IT WAY FORWARD.

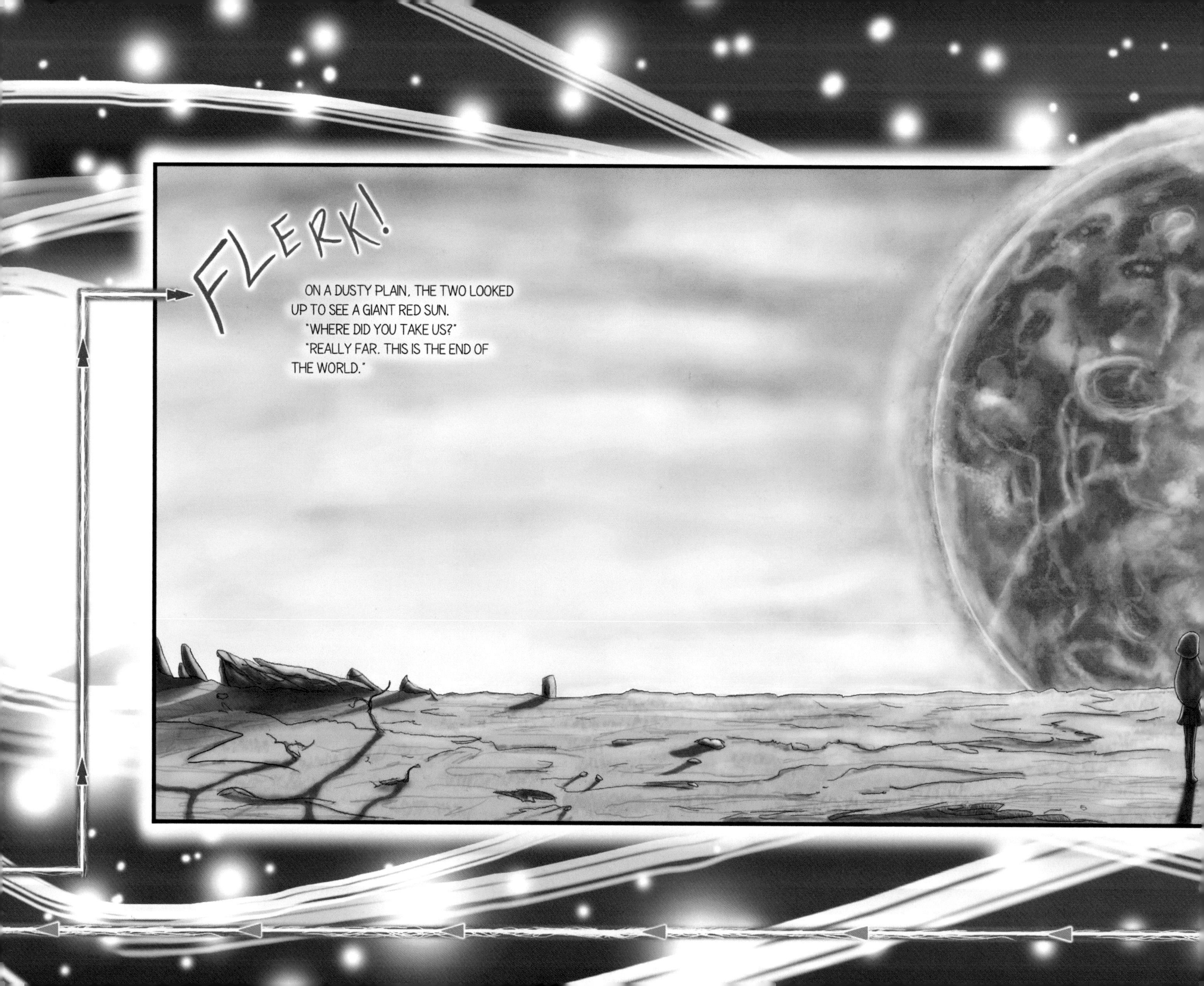
FLERK!
ON A DUSTY PLAIN, THE TWO LOOKED UP TO SEE A GIANT RED SUN.
"WHERE DID YOU TAKE US?"
"REALLY FAR. THIS IS THE END OF THE WORLD."

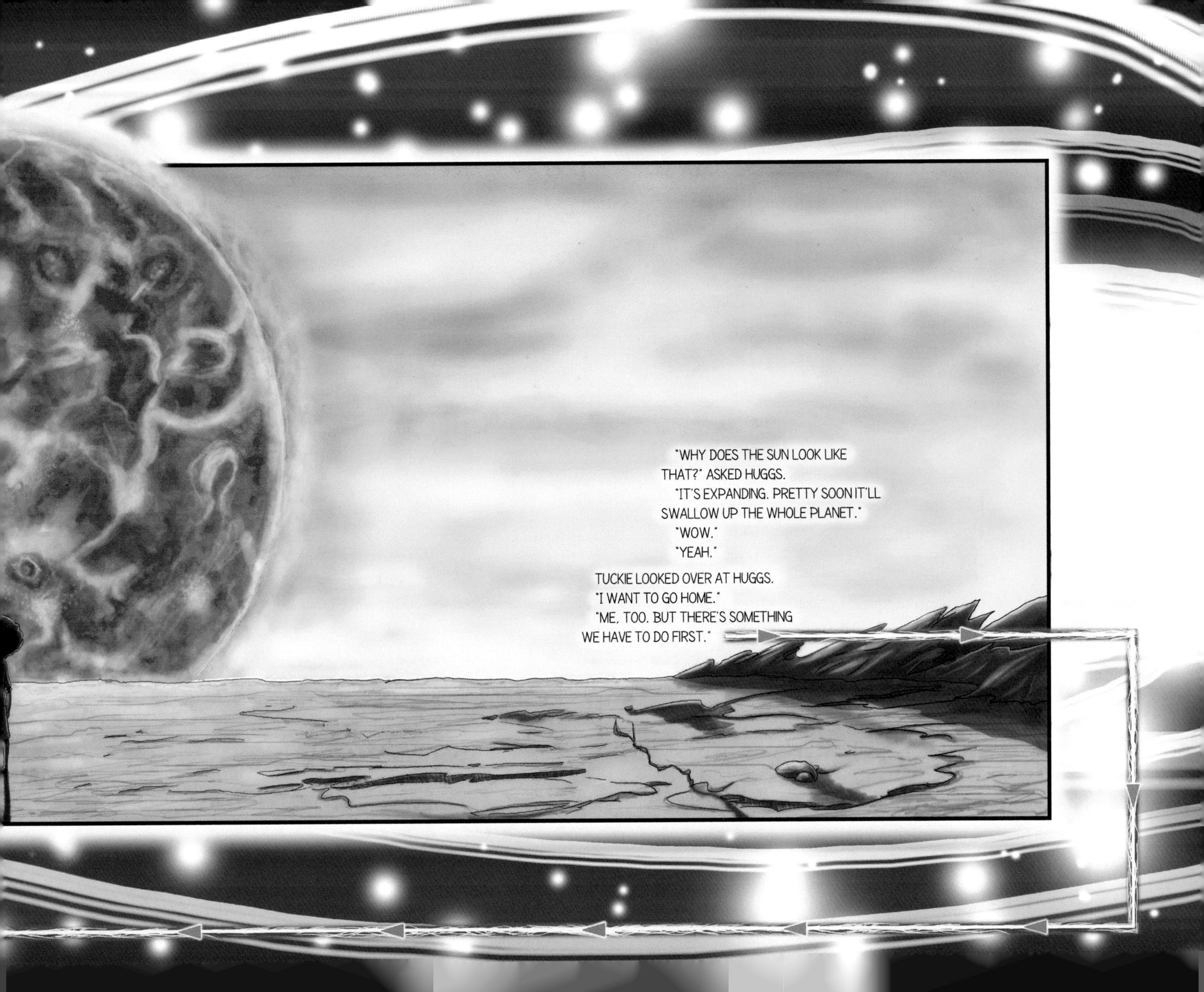

"WHY DOES THE SUN LOOK LIKE THAT?" ASKED HUGGS.

"IT'S EXPANDING. PRETTY SOON IT'LL SWALLOW UP THE WHOLE PLANET."

"WOW."

"YEAH."

TUCKIE LOOKED OVER AT HUGGS.

"I WANT TO GO HOME."

"ME, TOO. BUT THERE'S SOMETHING WE HAVE TO DO FIRST."

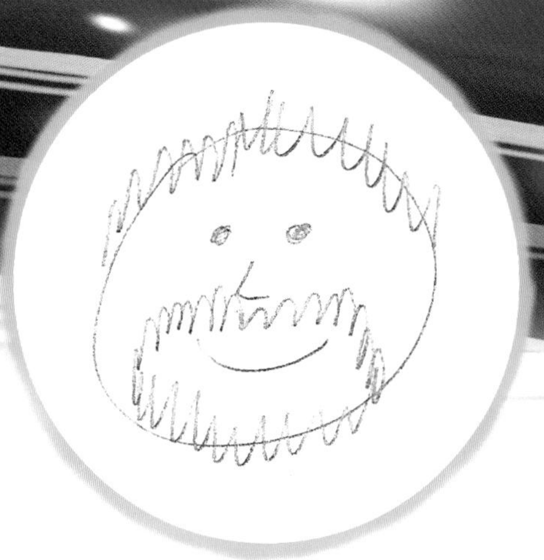

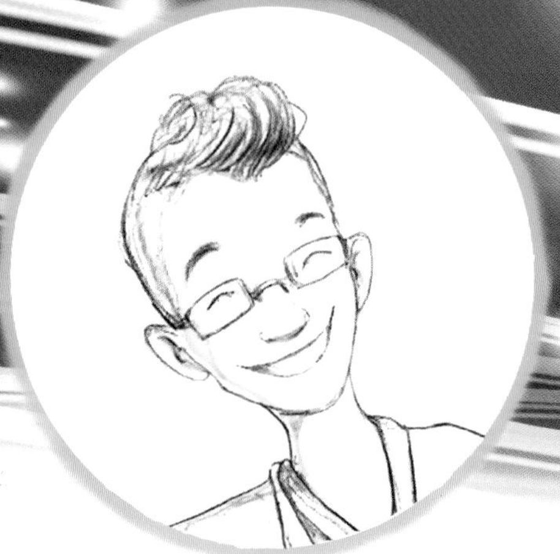

MATT BRENNAN

HAS ALWAYS BEEN **OBSESSED** WITH TIME TRAVEL, WHETHER IT'S ALTERING THE PAST IN ORDER TO CHANGE THE FUTURE, OR A CLOSED TIME LOOP WHERE EVERYTHING THAT'S GOING TO HAPPEN HAS ALREADY HAPPENED. HE LIVES IN BURBANK, CA WITH A STUFFED KLINGON TARG. THIS IS HIS FIRST BOOK.
SAY HI AT MATTARAMA.MB@GMAIL.COM

JONATHAN REICH

ALSO LIVES IN BURBANK, JUST BY COINCIDENCE, WHERE HE SCHEMES AND MAKES ART FOR KIDS, MOVIES, SCIENCE, AND THE INTERNET. HE **LOVES** PERIOD PIECES AND MAKING NEW CHARACTERS. THIS IS HIS FIRST BOOK TOO!
YOU CAN SEE MORE OF HIS WORK AT WWW.JONATHANREICH.ART

ISBN 978-0-692-12587-8 (HARDCOVER EDITION)

FRONT COVER IMAGE, BOOK DESIGN AND ILLUSTRATIONS BY JONATHAN REICH

PRINTED AND BOUND IN THE UNITED STATES OF AMERICA
FIRST PRINTING JUNE 2018
PUBLISHED BY INGRAM CONTENT GROUP, LA VERGNE, TN, USA

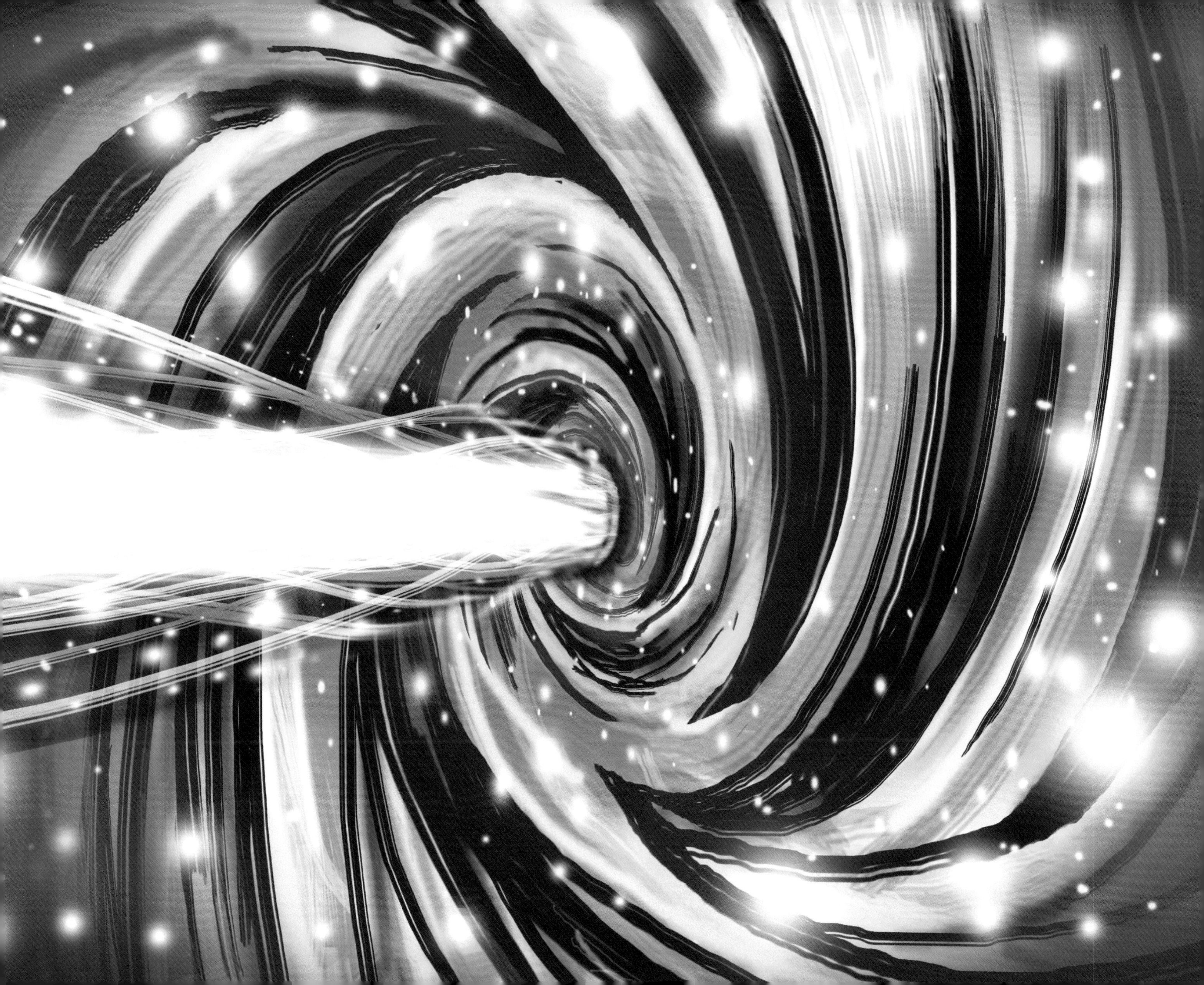

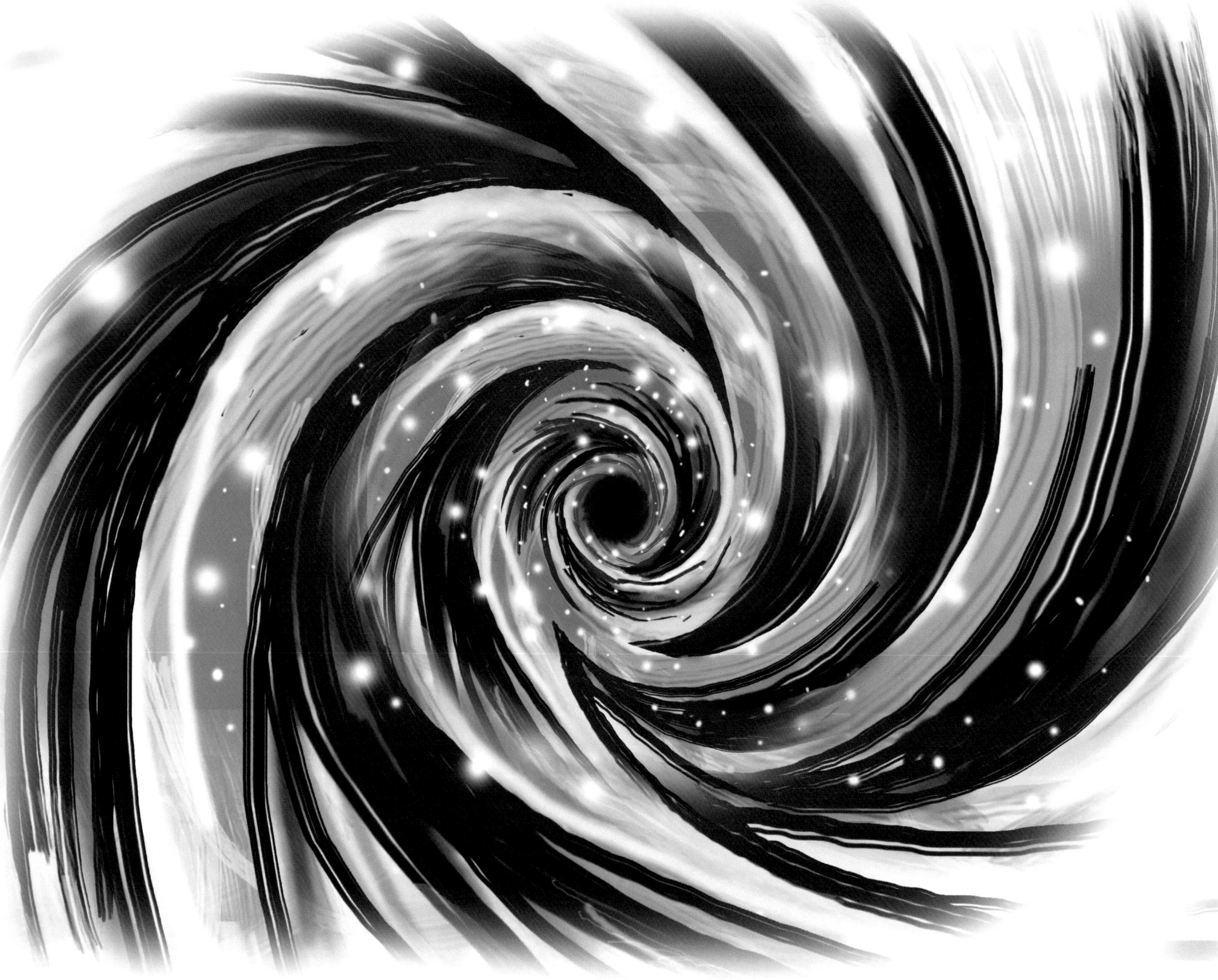

CPSIA information can be obtained at www.ICGtesting.com
Printed in the USA
BVIW120823051118
532193BV00011B/57